DEVASTATION

BRETT ARMSTRONG

Published by Expanse Books,
an imprint of Scrivenings Press LLC
15 Lucky Lane
Morrilton, Arkansas 72110
https://ExpanseBooks.pub

Printed in the United States of America

Paperback ISBN 978-1-64917-420-8

eBook ISBN 978-1-64917-421-5

Editors: Erin R. Howard and Linda Fulkerson

Map by Eric Dotseth.

Cover by Linda Fulkerson, bookmarketinggraphics.com

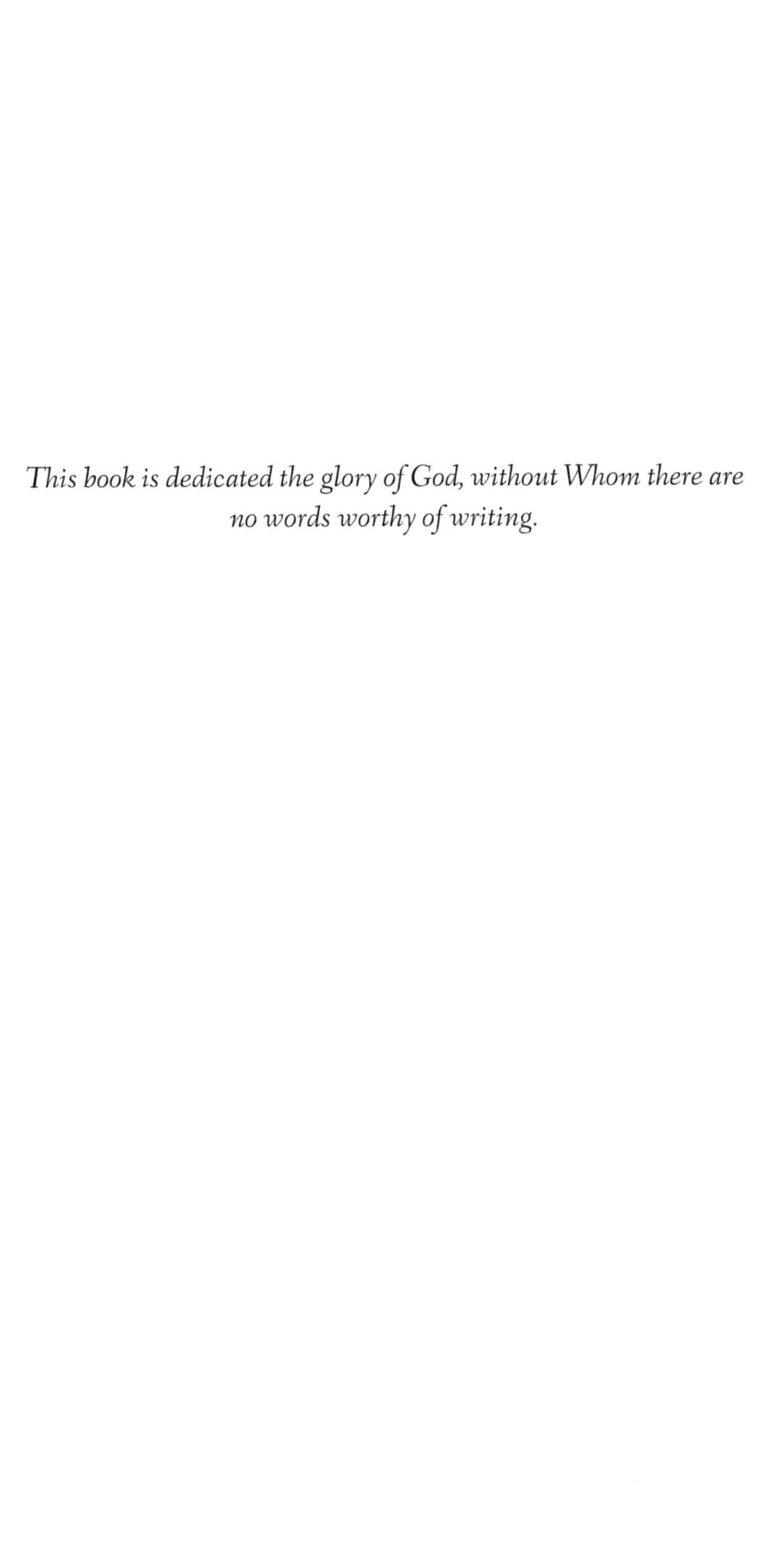

This book is dedicated the glory of God, without Whom there are no words worthy of writing.

MÔROER SEA
Last Landing
Hoarcrest
REÒTA FOREST
Wyvares
UPPER ALBAR MOUNTAINS
CALOON FOREST
IARAN
Manor Rock
EARAN
Keplan
Meadowbend
CAROON RIVER
FOGSHROUD STRAIT
Langlan's Lighthouse
EIGH RIVER
TREIGL MOUNTAINS
Caldoness
Langlan's Bay
Seabridge
LOCH CENDESLAS
Nottinburgh
Avon-caroon
Kilkern's Redoubt
GLOWER RIVER
KEYSTONE LAKES
Inkwell
STONE RIVER
WOLF GLEN
CAPE FINNGRATH
Glowerrethes
WOLFSGLEN RIVER
AVERBY FOREST
Hardoak
Airgid Mine
HILBREGH'S FOREST
LOWER ALBAR MOUNTAINS
Iarann Mine
Leiroc
Baileòrna
BRAIRD LOCH
ANNAMHAID SEA
LOCH SEUMAS
Dirkforge
ORTHALL RIVER
Cuan Cove
TOBIN'S COPSE
Fiswe Fens
LOCH ANGUS
ERMER RIVER
Seven Peaks
Ruins of Glastonae
Daggerpointe
NIGHV'S COPSE
GLASTON RIVER
BAY OF BRIS
ALESSIA INLET
Bris
AMBER STEPPE
BRADDEN RIVER
RUSH CREEK
Briscall
COASTAL FOREST
FINNEL LAKES
Estonbury
BRACKEN FOREST
Albarn

AN EXCERPT FROM THE LEGENDARIUM OF DRAGONS

BY FRANCIS DUBOIS, PHD

"More than one culture of the Lowlands bears tales of exotic, ferocious reptiles known colloquially as wyverns and dragons. An equal number of cultures also claim descendency from the lost and fable-shrouded land of Tislatna. Piecing together an accurate portrayal of what did and did not occur in that Ancient Era society may be impossible due to temperaments incurred by such groups as the Palatini Lucis Aeternae, or Knights of Light, less formally. I have, nonetheless, endeavored to piece together what might be seen as an accurate portrayal of the final days of Tislatna and its involvement with mysterious dragonkind.

"By all accounts, the Lost Realm of Tislatna was magnificent. A civilization so great that its wisdom and achievements are as yet unparalleled to this day, though we are thousands of years from its tragic destruction. Artifacts from cultures claiming descent piece together a picture of a people that captured the terrible and savage lizards, known as wyverns, and tamed them. Using arts now lost to history, they were able to transform them into thinking, reasoning, creatures capable of great things. These sentient creatures of might and mind were known as dragons. Though larger and more imposing in their brightly feathered forms, dragons still obeyed the whims of their masters. As seen over the Eras, petty rivalries, and competitions led to factions within Tislatna's highest echelons, eventually culminating in a destructive war that destroyed the island and its beloved beasts.

"As forementioned, the Knights of Light carry a far different accounting of Tislatna's fall. Attributing the creation of dragons to dark sorceries that fused the vicious and terrifying mystical creatures termed 'goblins' with wyvern beasts to create dragons. They contend that these dragons were more than sentient, more than sapient; they were malevolent, and the evil they infused into the men who created them spurred the purported High King of All Realms to destroy the island, its dragonkind, and all traces of the heretical magics which conjured dragons. It bears without saying but shall be repeated that this historian finds the fanciful myths of the Knights of Light interesting to read but of little value for real scholarship. However, as discoveries of lost material culture from Tislatna continue to surface and the continued mention of wyverns and dragons perpetuated into the Middle Era, including Ecthelowall's War for Restoration, the reader may apply a discerning eye to the evidence and derive his or her own informed conclusions."

1

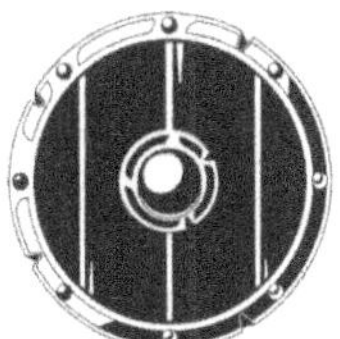

"I t's no use. We've lost another soldier," Thomas lamented. The teen sighed as he rose from where he'd just crouched, checking the Albaron soldier, who only continued shivering and looking into the distance. "Pale as snow, hands, feet, and eyes all ringed with the blackening. He definitely has it."

Fifty out of two hundred men in this company had fallen victim to the mysterious illness referred to in whispers by some as "The Devastation." Others called it "Ilyron's Hammer." Whatever name one gave it, for the Restoration's Army, the Devastation had come to mean one thing—death.

With a strained groan, the other man straightened from where he had examined a similarly stricken soldier. "Fifty-two. These two over here came down with it yesterday and already fading."

Behind the black hood-like mask and goggled eye holes, the physician William looked deceptively more sinister than those he treated. Adjusting his wide brim hat, also black, he raised his dark leather gloved hand and gestured to the tent's exit flap with a ghoulish silent insistence.

Outside the tent, Thomas was able to remove his frightful head covering and breathe in the fresh air of the moor. Before them stretched Kilkern's Redoubt. A strong Albaron breeze coming off the sea and sweeping through the verdant heather and puce thistle enveloped him. From atop the Redoubt's dark stony outcropping, Thomas had more than once found this place to be imbued with a tragic beauty.

Tragic, because it wasn't the castle looming behind them that kept them safe. Castle Kilkern boasted thick stone walls and jagged spires that blended well with the mountainous backdrop that typified Albaron. It had once withstood a two-year-long siege. Years ago, centuries ago. Before cannons and mortars and all the dread force of Monarch Ilyron's devastating war machine rendered it merely a target to pummel into powder. No, they weren't in danger here, but only because this was where the wounded and sick had been assembled. The Monarchists wouldn't be immune to the sickness that bore their master's name.

"How bad is it?" Thomas asked as William came up beside him, solemnity etched deeply into the Albaron's face.

"Worse than we can stand. But better than the heart of winter. Spring brought with it a flicker of hope."

"Let's not waste time speaking in code, good physician." Thomas turned his gaze squarely on the other man. They were roughly the same height, but the steely grey beard and wild wispy tangles of the William's hair betrayed the great gulf in experience between them.

"Unless the Libertians, you, and the Viceroy were able to add significantly more pressure in the south or this disease stops ravaging Albaron's armies ... we won't see the summer."

Thomas ran a hand through his thick brown hair. "Thank you for being blunt."

"You did ask for it." William carefully began removing the rest of his protective attire. Shedding his dark cloak, he revealed the brazen blue of his people. His silky tunic betrayed that he was far more than a physician. As an aged cousin of Albaron's highest noble, the Laird Ringan clan Loch, William was Steward of Kilkern, the ruler of this area. Embroidered on his tunic was the golden Clach, the fabled ram that led a tribe of Ecthel explorers deep into the mountains of Albaron to found their nation more than a thousand years ago. Whenever Thomas saw it, he could scarcely fight the gnawing ache inside him. There was a potent temptation to shed a tear for Steward William Kilkern the Physician, who would rather be among his people as a servant than a master. And for the pride-filled land symbolized in the stern ram's portrait as it teetered on the precipice of ruin. And for its people who fought to keep Ecthelowall from descending further into the depths of darkness to which Monarch Ilyron would drag it and all the Lowlands, if given the chance.

"You cannot wear such melancholy around the Baroness," William reminded him. His stout resolution the very sort of rebuke Thomas needed at such moments.

"It's no use to pretend. The Baroness sees straight through me. She always has."

This earned a knowing smile from the Steward, who clapped his hands on Thomas's shoulders and gave them a hearty shake. "Love reveals much. But it also hopes still more than it knows in this world."

Albarons were surprisingly a romantic people despite their gruff exteriors. Stark but beautiful in their way, not unlike the land in which they dwelt. Perhaps that was why Steward Kilkern was one of the few to whom Thomas had revealed his secret courtship. "I wouldn't, for the expanse of the Lowlands, let Mia think I've lost all hope."

Much as he did with William, Thomas could not bring himself to stick with formal honorifics. Not when he and Mia had grown up together, and especially not after they had grown together in the many months past as they fled the murderous Monarch and his forces. They had come so close to death so many times in their eighteen years of life. Both lost so much, enough to almost drive Mia to a bitter desperate end. But he had been there for her and she him in those darkest hours.

"I wouldn't think that you're allowed ta'," William replied, his thick burr showing as his expression turned conspiratorial. "Sir Thomas Fenwrest, heroic Knight of Light, you bear the banner of the High King. If you do no' rally us all to hope, who will?"

"Oh, please. Don't swell his head any further than it's already become," a strident voice, struggling to make the transition from tones of boy to man, called out. Gregor had snuck up on them. His arms were crossed, but more in dramatic protest than actual indignation. "Isn't it enough I have to see the Baroness swooning over him?"

"Cousin Gregor, are you really accusing me of having become conceited?" Thomas gave a poignant nod to the lavish outfit Gregor now wore.

"Mm-hmm. The lad does look to be settling into his role as Heir Apparent to Ecthelowall's throne quite comfortably."

Gregor rolled his eyes. "Over pert as you are, you're both lucky I'm about as likely to live to become Monarch as you are to actually win a game of bastions against me."

Thomas grimaced. Gregor was the most suitable candidate to take Ecthelowall's archaic title and throne, more so than Maldes Ilyron, who had usurped rule of Ecthelowall from his father, the Viceroy Ecthelion, and overturned the

Commonwealth. As a rival claimant, it made the younger teen both a target and a beacon for the Restoration effort. Even as the likelihood of restoring Viceroy Ecthelion became an ever more ethereal hook to hang hopes upon.

Gregor scowled, seeming to realize his humor had gone too far. "Sorry. It's just all a bit much."

Thomas walked over to his cousin. Gregor's head hung, looking dejectedly at the tent of the ill and dying. It was remarkable how much the events on the Isle of Geists had transformed Gregor. Once insufferable, now only occasionally a boor. Sir Hurstwell would've been proud to see the change. Were he still with them, he'd no doubt know just what to say to buoy their spirits.

But he wasn't. Which meant Thomas had to do his best in memory of his mentor. Nudging Gregor with his elbow, Thomas said, "Come on Your Highness. It wouldn't be fair for us to deny Mia a daily dose of your effervescent wit."

A sharp retort looked ready to launch from Gregor's lips when a rider on horseback galloped up to them and leapt down from his horse. He strode straight past the teens to Kilkern.

"Your Honor," he addressed him with a typical Albaron gesture of obeisance.

The steward waved back in acknowledgment. "Bodde, what news do you bring?"

"Ill, I'm afraid, Your Honor. A Monarchist fleet of ships landed on the shores west of here about an hour ago. They're disembarking troops now and look ready to march against you before dawn!"

2

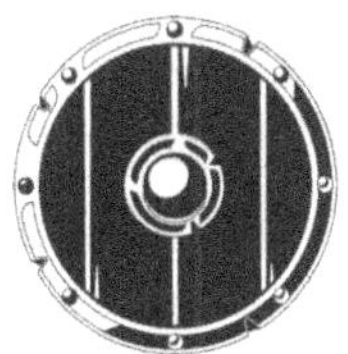

Within the walls of the castle, it was a normal temperate day in the month of Blomsen. Late-spring was treating them kindly even if events were not. Thomas could see from the ease with which everyone walked and buoyant banter within the market that word had not yet spread of the impending attack. Any minute a horn would blow to share that warning both to those bustling about the castle courtyard and in the city below, shattering the tranquility.

Kilkern's Redoubt was perched on the top of Ourst Hills. Wrapped around by the outer curtain wall, the city foundations straddled each mountainside of the valley. Twin sister keeps on each ridgetop boasted commanding views of the whole region. There would be no evacuations needed, but women, children, and the elderly would have to prepare for potential fires and seek refuge in the inner curtain walls and keeps. Every able-bodied man was required by Albaron law to report for service in the defense. Under normal circumstances, that would be a formidable force to call up. However, the Devastation had already greatly diminished those capable of mounting the defense, and many more were away on other battlefields of the war.

Thomas only had a few minutes to do what he had to before he would be missed at the muster call. He had to get to Mia before the siege started because he knew tomorrow's sunrise would find this castle reduced to rubble and those within its walls dead or captives of the Monarch.

Telling himself over and over it wasn't selfish, Thomas half believed it. Truth was, Mia and Gregor needed to escape for the good of Ecthelowall. But for that good or not, he couldn't let them be swept away.

Passing by the western keep guards with a salute, he made his way through the expansive entry area to the grounds at the back of the structure. A terraced garden grew on the slopes. Often, he would find her tending to the little patch of Emeral thistle growing here, because it reminded her of her home. A home she could not return to unless this war was won.

There was no sign of Mia.

"Perhaps she's in her quarters?" Gregor offered, breaking the tense silence.

She wasn't the type to stay inside the keep all day, but if she was about the grounds, surely he would've spotted her by now. Nodding, Thomas started toward her chambers, struggling to move as fast as possible without appearing too hurried. But it was fruitless. Even the maidens assigned to attend to her were absent.

Where can she be?

Perhaps sensing Thomas's tension as they stalked back outside, Gregor spoke up again, "You know, I've made lots of progress in swordsmanship practice since you last watched."

"Really?" Thomas replied, almost thoughtlessly, as he wove around the busied interior of the castle's grounds.

"Captain Luach says if I keep this up, I could be ready to join the War of Restoration before summer solstice."

Thomas came to a complete halt and whirled around to face Gregor. "You're not going to fight in this war!"

Gregor's eyes widened. He looked so much like a whipped pup, it snuffed out the blaze of Thomas's anger before it could fully catch.

He sighed. His tone had been harsh. Taking his younger cousin by the shoulders, he tried again in a gentler manner. "We've been over this. Your role in all this is to stay safe. Stand at the ready to help guide the country to a better future when the war ends and the time to rebuild Ecthelowall begins."

What am I saying? If I don't find Mia and get them both on horses riding away from here, they won't live to see the week's end, let alone that sort of future.

Walking again, Thomas didn't bother to look back as Gregor launched into a familiar argument about his place in things. Letting the other teen grouse, Thomas stalked up to another guard, who had apparently gotten notice of what was coming because he was assisting with rolling a defensive cannon in place. "Sergeant, may I have a word?"

The older man sneered down his long nose and wagged his bristly grey mustache. "What is it, boy? I have things to be about!"

The soldier's dim brown eyes widened as he seemed to finally focus. "Oh, it's you, Sir Fenwrest. And Your Honor," he amended, straightening to give an Albaron salute of sorts.

"Thank you, Sergeant," Gregor replied with some of the old airs of authority he could put on that still irked Thomas.

Gritting his teeth, Thomas cut in before Gregor could speak again. "I know about the impending attack. I'm looking for Baroness Sornfold. But I can't find her or her attendants."

The old Sergeant's bushy brows raised in concern as

though he felt the frustration radiating off Thomas. "I dare say that is because I saw her and one of her attendants heading down to the death tents—er—the field hospital."

"What?" Thomas demanded, not properly masking his concern. How was he supposed to? She could fall ill with the Devastation, and then he and Ecthelowall would lose her. Of the two, he felt certain he would feel the loss so much more deeply.

"It's not proper for a Lady such as herself to visit so somber a venue." Gregor stepped in. Somehow, he escaped the petulance he'd indulged in a moment before, transforming with ease into a budding diplomat. "Who approved such a thing?"

"Why, I heard Steward Kilkern himself encourage her to visit the tents. I believe one of her attendants fell ill this morning and was carried down there."

"Thank you, Sergeant. Back to your duties." Gregor returned the Albaron salute.

Thomas didn't bother with the gesture. He was already dashing back down to the lower courtyard, intending to storm the tents and find Mia.

"Thomas, what about the attack? As captain of the Baroness's guard, you have to join the muster with the others in defense of the castle." Gregor struggled to keep up with Thomas.

Ignoring him, Thomas moved faster. There wasn't time to argue with Gregor over what constituted the proper manner of safeguarding Mia.

With a surprising burst of speed, Gregor dashed ahead and cut off Thomas's path. Gregor was getting faster, but Thomas easily whirled around him and kept going.

"You know you keep acting like this, and they're going to see through your 'noble bodyguard act' and force you two to break up."

Skidding to a halt, Thomas faced Gregor, who stood huffing about ten feet back. He glowered at him. They were out in the open, but no one was in the immediate vicinity to have heard. Blabbing like that could ruin things for him and Mia.

"The least you could do after I've done more than my share to keep the secret is hear me out once in a great while!" Gregor spat in accusation.

The biting comment sobered Thomas. Hard as it was to admit, Gregor was actually the one being mature and level-headed at the moment. Thomas drew in a deep breath. "You're right. But time is tight. I can't chance something happening to Mia."

Gregor seemed to chew on that for a bit. "We're in public—it's Baroness Sornfold."

"Right. Baroness Sornfold. Thank you." Thomas didn't have to feign gratitude.

"Well, lead on."

They were just a few dozen yards from the gate back to the hospital tents when it occurred to him that the steward must have known he was sending Mia into danger.

A loud blast from a ram's horn sounded from the top of the keep, reverberating through the hillsides. He was out of time.

3

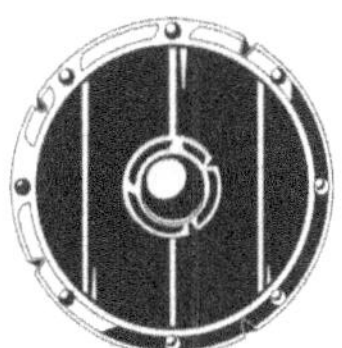

"Stay here and wait for me." Thomas made it three steps before feeling a tug at his arm.

"No," Gregor insisted. "I'm coming with you!"

There wasn't time for Thomas to stay and fight over the matter. Rather than waste the energy, he muttered, "Keep up." He dashed past the protesting guards to the gatehouse as the first of those outside the castle walls began streaming inside.

Thomas wove through the press of people, pushing toward the tents with the ill.

Why in the Lowlands would Steward Kilkern send Mia here knowing the castle would soon be under siege?

The thought turned over and over in his head without resolution. It made no sense. Especially given the steward's otherwise imminently keen insights and planning.

"Slow up," Gregor mewled, farther behind than before.

"You insisted on coming." Thomas slowed. A minute later they were at the outskirts of the medical camp. A pair of soldiers strode to intercept them.

"You there. By order of the steward, no one is allowed to

13

come near the sick. There is an imminent attack by Monarchist armies. You must turn back and shelter within the castle walls."

"What nonsense," Gregor complained. "We were just here earlier. Why would visiting the ill comport with sheltering in the castle?"

"They don't want anyone bringing the ill into the castle for safety," Thomas surmised, grimly. It was pragmatic and tragic in one.

The soldier nodded, "My orders are simply to turn back any who comes. Especially whiney children." He shot Gregor a pointed a look.

Before Gregor could snap back at the guard, Thomas gripped his shoulder and spoke up, "We respect your orders, but I'm the Captain of Baroness Sornfold's guard, and I was told the steward had sent her to this camp. I need to bring her safely into the castle before the siege begins."

The guard nodded as if finally recognizing Thomas and Gregor. "Of course. The steward left explicit instructions regarding you both. He said to make sure you two in particular are not allowed into the camp and to escort you back to the main gates personally."

Gregor shot Thomas a startled look. "What? Why in the Lowlands would he do that?"

Thomas kept silent and appraised the obstructive guard cooly. Something was very wrong. But what?

The soldier drew his sword, as did his compatriot. "Get to walking Ecthels," he ordered.

Thomas backed up a few steps, pushing Gregor behind him. "There's been a serious misunderstanding," he said, keeping his voice calm and level. His eyes roved between each sword pointing at them.

"The misunderstanding is you Ecthels bringing your war into

Albaron's lands and then acting like you rule over us. We didn't join your War of Restoration to help your Viceroy—we joined it to make sure your Monarch never attempts to take our lands.

"So, I will say it once more. Leave or I don't care who you are—I will cut you down where you stand!"

Thomas worked his tongue over his teeth, struggling against the urge to brandish his sword and strike down the soldier. Thomas knew the High King wouldn't want him to attack. This soldier was short-sighted but not evil. An obstacle but not an enemy. At least not openly. Taking another step back, Thomas raised his hands placatively. "Very well. We can see ourselves back to the gate."

"Thomas?" Gregor protested after they had walked out of ear shot for the soldiers. "If we don't get the Baroness out of there, she could be captured or worse!"

"I know that, Gregor," Thomas snapped before reining in his frustration. "I know. We have to make a circuitous approach. Come around from another side and sneak into the camp."

"Another side? All the approaches have guards posted," Gregor protested, but he followed Thomas as he veered away from the gates and ducked behind a particularly thick patch of bushes and briars.

"Not the eastern face of the camp," Thomas corrected.

"Well, of course, because the hill was excavated there to expand the camp. It's a sheer drop, almost a cliff!"

Grumbling as he went, Thomas retorted, "If you have a better way to warn *the Baroness* in time to deliver her from Monarch Ilyron's forces, then I'd love to hear it."

At the edge of the steep embankment, rocks clattered off the rough, freshly hewn stone overlooking the encampment. Gregor looked up at Thomas, incredulous. A bit of his old whiney tone strangled his words. "Literally anything is a better idea than plummeting to our deaths here."

"Not helping," Thomas chided. As he evaluated the situation with the cliff side, he could see Gregor's point. It would be risky to scale the cliff on a good day without rushing. This was not a good day.

Another blast from the horn reverberated through the air.

Good day or not, he would scale a cliff face a hundred times the size of this and ride a thousand leagues to help Mia. One day, he would have to let her go so she could take her place among the regal and magnificent. Until that day, he needed her. They had been through so much together. They had helped each other survive what most would only ever dream of in their worst nightmares. Dangerous or not, he was climbing down this cliff.

Gnawing on his lip, Thomas dithered only a moment longer. "Stay here." He swung his legs over the edge. Lowering himself, he probed for his first foothold.

"You're mad if you think I'm going to wait around here to watch you fall to your death," Gregor snapped, his voice cracking. An instant later, he was alongside Thomas, grimacing as tiny shards of stone skittered to the bottom. Gregor wasn't exaggerating the possible outcome of this.

Thomas immediately realized gripping the stony facing wasn't going to be as simple as he expected. The places for him to hold were shallow and required a tight grip. He glanced at Gregor. The boy's knuckles were white. Each time he changed the positioning of his feet, he had to support his full weight briefly with only his arms as his foot probed for a place of refuge.

They moved slowly, too slowly.

Sometimes sideways for several feet before finding a reasonable way down. If the growing aches and uncertainties of their descent were as potent for Thomas as they were for Gregor, then he wasn't sure how his younger cousin was managing at all.

Twenty-five feet to go, and faint tremors raced the length of his arms. Checking on Gregor again his eyes widened with horror. Gregor's whole body was shaking, and Thomas could see his hands were slipping. If he lost all hold and fell from this height, he'd be dead. Even if he survived the initial impact, he would have to be taken to a physician, which meant coming in closer contact with the Devastation.

Thomas had to do something. Immediately. But what? He was barely holding on himself. Why had he been such a fool and risked this? It was one thing to put himself in danger, but how had he accepted such a thing for Gregor? He was just a boy. No, more than that, he was an heir to a lineage that was the rallying banner of the Restoration. Yes, the Restoration was to depose Ilyron and restore Ecthelion as Viceroy, but even Thomas knew it was temporary. There was a reason Ilyron's bid for the monarch's throne had resonated with so many. The greatness of the past was a temptation, and Ecthelion would inevitably abdicate. Gregor was all that remained, the last unsevered tether to a past to which many longed to return.

A strangled cry escaped Gregor's lips as his grip faltered.

4

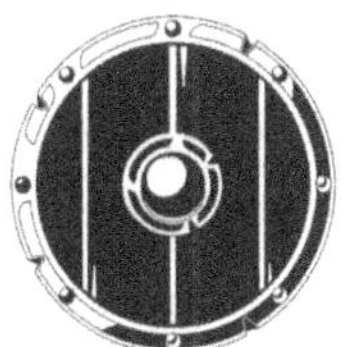

There was no time to think. No time to plan, Thomas's heart pleaded, "Help us, Great King!" He lunged over and grabbed Gregor's hand. His fingers closed over Gregor's just before he fell beyond reach. Thomas felt his other hand give. They were both falling.

Thomas's hand scrambled for anything, any tiny ledge with enough purchase to hang onto. His fingers skidded along the stones finding nothing. A desperate plea, incoherent except in its feverous depth welled within him. They were only twelve feet from the ground. Thomas closed his eyes.

A sudden jerk sent a jolt through Thomas's frame and he barely kept a hold on Gregor. His hand was fixed fast to the most unlikely of outcroppings. He couldn't even feel his fingers, but they held and as the pain screamed within his shoulders from the strain. Gregor flailed and grabbed hold of the cliff wall farther down, his smaller hands hungrily grasping once more to the stone.

Thomas found his footing and gave himself a few jagged breaths space to strain out, "Thank you! Thank you, my King!"

They struggled down the remaining distance. Thomas didn't feel able to breathe until their feet were firmly on the rock-strewn ground. As he looked upward, he struggled to hold himself together as joy surged into the space evacuated by his fear and guilt for precious seconds before he needed to refocus.

Gregor was trembling, and Thomas knew there was a chance the stress of everything might be putting him into shock. Before he could sort out just how to tend to the younger Fenwrest, Gregor's shudders stilled. He looked up at Thomas, eyes wide with wonder. "The King of Light. He rescued us, didn't He?"

Without hesitation, Thomas nodded. "He did."

His cousin didn't say anything at first. Those young eyes, so like Thomas's uncle's, were trained thoughtfully on the cliff face for almost longer than Thomas knew they could spare before Gregor said, "That's thrice now He's delivered us from an impossible situation."

"More than that," Thomas corrected gently. He placed a hand on the boy's shoulder when the pain forced him to drop the arm and nurse it gingerly. "Ah."

"You're hurt?" Gregor asked, looking concerned.

"Mm. When we jerked to a stop—" was all he could grind out before he got a hold of the pain.

Once more, Gregor looked thoughtful, like he wanted very much to say something but couldn't quite get it out. He finally voiced one word, "Why?"

Thomas let out a breath in a rush. Already they were too tight on time. "Later," he promised. "We have to get Mia out of here."

Gregor nodded. Then, as if climbing out of his pensiveness, snorted. "Not going back up that way, though."

For an instant, Thomas could smirk. "Definitely not." He stalked hurriedly toward the tents nearest them.

"Cover your mouth with your shirt and keep outside the tents," he instructed.

"I know, I know. Steward Kilkern's told me enough times himself."

Going among the tents, though Knights of Light had seemingly shown to be immune to the Devastation, Thomas covered his face with his tunic as well. The stench of those dead and those swiftly on their way to it was horrid. They had checked eleven of the sprawling tents before they ducked into one with low lamps burning. Among the ill were two women, one of whom was bending over a patient whispering something.

"Mia!" Thomas crossed the space in a few strides to embrace her.

As he wrapped his arms around her, he felt her jump in surprise. After a breath's space, she faced him and beamed him a sly grin visible even from under a veil she wore to keep her face covered. "Hale evening to you as well. Normally, you aren't so bold about displaying affection in front of others ... I think I could get used to greetings like this."

He pulled back to survey the room and saw that they were alone apart from a stolid woman from the Vogteremark with hair so light it was almost silver, even in the lamplight. She did not stir on his arrival. Such quiet, unassuming personality and stalwart posturing were familiar. Though she looked down at one of the ill, a flaxen braid obscuring her face, Thomas recognized Mia's maiden in waiting, Ilsa. The maiden had glimpsed enough since coming into Mia's service to know Thomas was more than the captain of the Baroness's guard. Trusting her was an afterthought.

There were also, of course, the ill. And with them the tragic truth that most wouldn't make it through the night to tell anyone about the embrace.

Mia gave a gentle toss of her head to move one of her

auburn curls out of her face. She arched a brow in question at him. Realizing he still was holding her quite close, he let his grip on her slip to just a loose hold on her hands. "Not if you keep risking yourself like this. What are you doing here?"

Mia's expression drifted from affection into annoyance. "Visiting those ill with this terrible disease. Just as you and Gregor did earlier today."

He scowled. The risk was different for him, but he certainly knew better than to bother arguing that at the moment. "Yes, but we didn't come out here while the castle is about to come under siege."

Her emerald eyes widened. "Under siege? What are you talking about?"

"Steward Kilkern received word while we were here that the Monarchists have landed an army nearby and are marching on the castle as we speak. Didn't you hear the horns?"

"I, well, yes, but ..." She glanced down at the patient she had been whispering to when Thomas arrived. He saw that she was her other maiden in waiting, Lorelei. The young woman's eyes were closed and ringed in black. Sweat shone on her forehead just beneath her matted brown locks, and her pallid lips were twisted in the grimace of a fever dream.

"I'm sorry," he mumbled, not sure what else to say. "But we must hurry. I have to get you and Gregor out of here."

Mia's brow furrowed and she glanced over at Lorelei. "I can't just leave her. She's been with me ever since we left Kirke."

"You have to go, my lady," Ilsa spoke up, her voice threaded with a subservience even as she insisted. "Those beasts cannot have you! I will stay and watch over Lorelei."

Thomas could see in Mia's eyes her conflict. A pettier version of her would have found the choice simple. That was before all they had endured. Beneath the mantle of her new title was a far greater change in the young woman. And he loved her the more for it, even if it vexed him that the new Mia would violate his impulse to safeguard her.

Mia's brow knitted and her mouth set in a hard line. Thomas already knew what she would say. "Ilsa, I cannot simply abandon you both."

Gregor cleared his throat. "Baroness, if anyone is lost here today, it cannot be you. Otherwise, all other losses will be for not."

Shooting a glare at the boy, she retorted, "You're one to talk. Shouldn't the Heir Apparent to the throne be safely behind the castle walls?"

"I'm here because of him," he responded hotly, a note of childish petulance tinging his words.

Thomas spoke up preemptively. "I know what you're going say."

"Do you?" Mia replied, raising her auburn brows. "Then why would you possibly do such a foolish thing?"

Gnawing on his lip, Thomas wrestled for an acceptable answer. One that wasn't what immediately came to mind. He looked from Mia to Gregor to Ilsa to Lorelei. All of them were close in age. Just youths. His gaze lingered, taking in Lorelei's shallow breaths and with each one a draught of truth about the brevity and uncertainty of life. "Because I love you, and I can't bear to lose you," he blurted out.

It took a moment to muster the courage to look Mia in the eyes. He had consciously broken his rule about openly acknowledging their relationship in the most brazen way possible. Mia's rich green eyes were glassy. She said nothing, so he couldn't tell for sure whether she was upset or enamored with his declaration.

He was all the more thrown as she cleared her throat and said, if quietly, "Then, I will go."

Relief flooded his chest. He reached out his hand to her and she took it with a gentle squeeze. She didn't have to say the words outright. The tender resilience of her touch sang the melody of her inner voice, "I love you too." Reading someone schooled to keep genuine emotions buried was often a challenge, so he appreciated the extra overture.

"No need to be running off, Your Honor," a less familiar voice intoned with mock graciousness.

At the entrance to the tent stood the annoying guard from earlier and two others, all with weapons drawn. "Wouldn't want you nor the Heir Apparent missing the Monarch's arrival."

5

___

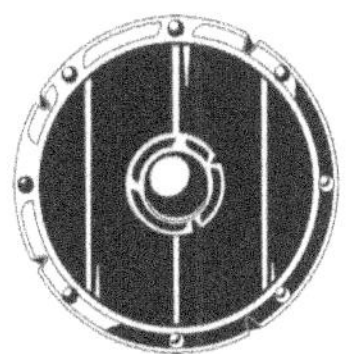

"You can't be serious," Gregor whined. "You're all traitors?"

The lead guard scowled at him. "Traitors? I'm Nevin, son of Garrel, and my family has lived under the Redoubt's shadow for two hundred years. You Ecthels send our men of Albaron to battlefields and bring that horrid Devastation upon our women and children so we're all dying for your foolish war? It would be treason not to purge your filth from our lands."

"Do you truly believe Ilyron will leave your lands once you've handed us over and the Restoration loses the war?" Mia asked, projecting with her newly assumed voice of authority. But Thomas saw the tension in her jaw, her posture. She was frightened.

"The Monarch promised as much," Nevin replied as he and the others sauntered toward them. "And if he doesn't, then we'll make him leave, just like we're doing with you leeches."

In a pair of deft movements, Thomas drew his spiritsword and moved in front of Mia, Gregor, and Ilsa. He leveled the point of the burning blade at the men. "You'll come no farther.

Hate us if you must, but you will not be handing the Baroness over to that monster. The Monarch isn't simply another ambitious despot. He has allied himself with evil and all that is in rebellion against the High King of All Realms."

At this, Nevin chuckled. "You don't say. Well, as it happens, I don't tend to think much of the 'high king' myself, then. The Monarchists are winning your war and you're hiding behind us as shields. If Monarch Ilyron is as wicked a screw as you claim, then your king must not be powerful enough to stop him."

That bit of reasoning brought Thomas up short. Ever since he had seen the vision of the High King and pledged his loyalty to him, he hadn't questioned his lord's power and prowess to bring about all he promised. Nor did he now—at least not for less than a breath's space. Gripping the fabric of his tunic over his chest plate, he said, "See this emblem of his Kingdom?"

"What? That goofy shiny lamb?" one of the three asked.

"No, I think it's supposed to be a rather austere lion," the one flanking Nevin corrected.

"It is both," Thomas asserted. "Forbearing, gentle for this brief moment, but in the end, he will reclaim the Lowlands with irresistible ferocity and rule them. Justice, order, peace, goodness—all will be the substance of his reign."

Thomas was not oblivious to the way the other men were spreading out, their short broad swords drawn. He wasn't about to let them flank him in bluster or battle. Even if the persistent twinge in his shield arm since their fall reminded him it wouldn't be as quick to respond as it should.

"It's always the same with you knights. Turning to the future, because you have nothing to show for yourselves in the present," another guard said with a sneer.

Angling to immediately intercept the closest of the trio, Thomas shook his head. "If you three won't listen to reason, then perhaps you'll heed the sight of fire." He brandished his blade, the flames crackling along its length. He could feel the flush of heat all the way up his arm and in his core.

The nearest guard looked puzzled. "What fire? You have some flint to set this tent ablaze, kill all the ill with the Devastation? That doesn't seem very knightly."

They couldn't see the flames coursing along the spiritsword's gleaming, sharp plane. Bungling into aiding evil, though they may be at the moment, they weren't either sufficiently devoted to the Great King or in full rebellion against him in order to see his fire. That was something, at least.

"Enough!" The lead guard charged at Thomas.

Whirling to face him, Thomas raised his round shield, engraved in burning script as well, and caught the blow. Barely. Deflecting it wide, Thomas made the best of it and pivoted to come around behind Nevin and strike him with the pommel of the spiritsword. Pain radiated along his shield arm. It wasn't the worst Thomas had felt. If this were his first battle, he might've faltered. But he was far from a novice now.

From Thomas's right, he glimpsed another of the group bearing down on him. The heavyset man brought his broadsword down hard and sent Thomas reeling backward as he narrowly deflected the attack.

Braided red bands of hair swinging, the Albaron pushed his advantage with quick, powerful strokes that kept Thomas backing up. Forcing Thomas toward the last of the trio who would be waiting for an easy kill.

But Thomas's foe was overcommitting to each blow. He swung high and Thomas anticipated it. Ducking under the swipe, Thomas stepped forward and struck the man square in the face with his fist.

Shaken up, the other man stumbled back, and Thomas battered him to the ground with his shield. A flicker of motion at his flank. He spun and intercepted another of the traitors coming at him. Holding the smaller, quicker fighter at bay with swift strokes of his sword, he called out, "Gregor, get Mia and Ilsa out of here!"

The younger teen snapped a response, but Thomas didn't catch it because he had to leap backward as Nevin picked himself up and joined his underling's latest sortie. Thomas swung his sword around, forcing Nevin back, and immediately brought up a hasty block from his shield to catch the attack from the other man.

The block was ready, but barely held, and Thomas stumbled, just managing to brace himself upright. From his new angle, he caught sight of Gregor, sword drawn, advancing on Nevin from the left. "Gregor, no!"

Thomas only glimpsed the sneer Nevin bore before he had to block another attack from his current opponent. That brute was going to skewer Gregor!

Marshaling his strength, he pushed off on the next attack with his shield. Teeth gritted against the pain that swelled with it, Thomas brought his spiritsword around. Once, twice, three times, hammering his burning blade down onto the other man's sword and shattering it like glass. Both fighters looked at the ruined weapon in shock. Thomas recovered and rushed his foe, battering him to the ground with his shoulder and then rendering him unconscious with a strike from his sword pommel.

Looking up from the defeated man, his breath caught. "Gregor, watch out!"

6

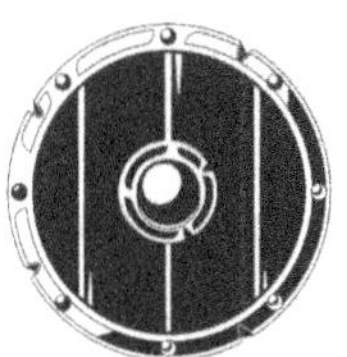

I f the boy heard, he was slow to listen and almost caught a scouring blow across his shoulder. His narrow defense earned him a nick and sent him to the ground. He scrambled back to his feet. The cruel guard was bearing down on him.

Surging forward, Thomas leaped between the two, his shield blocking Gregor's feeble and frantic counter as Thomas stepped in to parry Nevin's imminent finishing blow.

Stunned, Nevin didn't have time to recover from the parry and took the brunt of a smash from Thomas's shield directly to the disgraced guard's face. Nevin stumbled and went down. Holding his face, he scrambled backward, much as Gregor had, but Thomas was on him. Pinning Nevin's sword down with his boot and pointing the burning tip of his spiritsword in the man's face, he ground out through aches radiating in his shoulder, "It's over," he said, with a tone as much instructive as informative.

The guard scowled up at Thomas and relinquished his hold on the sword, holding his hands up placatively. "That it seems. For now."

"Mia," Thomas called, his eyes still on the man. "Bring me something to bind him. We'll leave him and the others on the road for their new master, the Monarch, to find."

"It's Baroness or Your Honor," Mia replied, her voice cold and hard as stone. "Ilsa, retrieve the needed cords for Captain Fenwrest."

"My lady," Ilsa managed to stammer out. Her eyes shot from the results of the furious struggle to Mia and back again before complying.

Thomas's brows furrowed as he gazed across the space at Mia, whose expression was impassive. Her emerald eyes refused to meet his. What had he done wrong?

A moment later, Ilsa approached with some rope they used for securing the worst of the patients when in need of surgery. She handed it to Thomas gingerly as though he himself were dangerous.

"Death to the Ecthel pigs!" the downed captain bellowed and drew a hidden dirk twisting up to bury it in Thomas's abdomen.

The blade glanced off, shredding Thomas's tunic and revealing the burning inscriptions on the silvery cuirass Thomas wore beneath. Thomas slammed the pommel of his sword down on top of the bewildered would-be assassin's head. Nevin dropped heavily to the ground.

"Thomas!" Mia gasped and was next to him in a moment. Her hands hovered near where his tunic was sliced and her eyes searched frantically for a wound. He would've received a grievous one were it not for the divinely imbued *Thorax Dikaiosyne*—in the ancient tongue, righteous cuirass—he wore. At length, her lips pursed, and she breathed out a sigh. "You're all right."

"It appears so." He put his hands on her arms, squaring himself to her. She looked up at him, the haunting remnants of her horror echoing to him like a banshee's cry in her expression. "Even I forget, the High King ever keeps watch over his Knights."

There was a tightening around her eyes, and she pulled back out of the embrace. Mia turned her attention to Gregor. Ilsa was tending to him. She had already retrieved a swath of cloth to press against his minor wound.

"Are you okay, Your Honor?" Mia's voice sounded off, strained, even with the mock reverence.

"I think I'll live. No thanks to Thomas," he grumbled.

"No thanks to me?" Thomas repeated. "You're kidding. I just saved you from being carved up like a Clearing Day pheasant."

Gregor was on his feet, his cheeks red as the berries often enjoyed with that pheasant. It was Mia who spoke first, though. "Maybe he's spent too much time watching you galivant around. He doesn't seem to respect danger, either."

Thomas gaped, unsure what to say or where this iciness had come from.

Ilsa broke the silence by cautiously reminding them, "My lady, you and his honor must go. The Monarchists are still on their way."

Thomas wasn't sure where Mia's ire was coming from, but, unfortunately, Ilsa was right. There was no time to sort that out or even linger a moment longer. They had to go. Shouldering the rope rather than bothering to tie up the bested guards, Thomas announced, "At your order, my lady. We'll exit the camp and make for Caldoness."

To Ilsa, he added, "I'm sorry, but I don't believe you can stay any longer. Lorelei will be cared for, even if and when the Monarchists take Kilkern's Redoubt. If these three are any indication, the Monarchists have those sympathetic to their cause deeply embedded here. They will no doubt try to use you to find Mia and Gregor."

Ilsa's eyes widened with dread, and her youthful lips twisted in indecision. "My lady?" she pleaded.

Mia placed a reassuring hand on her shoulder, "Captain Fenwrest ... Thomas ... is right. Lorelei would want you safe."

"And, um, I could use a nurse on the journey," Gregor added. "The Baroness and the captain don't have the same tender spirit of a healer as you do."

Oh, really?

Ilsa tilted her head to regard Gregor, her expression unreadable. She clasped her hands in front of her and nodded in deferral. "As you wish, Your Honor."

Taking stock of his charges, Thomas decided he'd given all the space and time they could afford, and then some. "Good. Stay close to one another, and let me keep a lead till we've mounted the horses and are underway. There could be other ... obstacles to our escape." He didn't want to go into details of the possibility that even the loyal Albarons might object vehemently to them slipping away. Though they may have been twisted and spiteful, the defeated guards were right. To some degree, Albaron was fighting this war on the Restoration's behalf and had already weathered many blows for it.

There were no other sentries, Monarchist or otherwise, posted at the camp of the ill. The group managed to make it about a third of the way up the path to the fortress before another long horn blast sounded.

Thomas froze in place.

No. No. No!

After more than a minute, Gregor called out, "Why are we just standing here like a herd of grazing sheep?"

"They've locked the gates to the outer wall. We can't get

into the Redoubt," Thomas replied, crestfallen. How had he messed up this badly?

"Why not? Surely, they wouldn't turn us away," Gregor protested.

Thomas sighed. "They wouldn't. But the stir from having the Baroness Sornfold and Heir Apparent Fenwrest walking up to the gates after they're locked would ensure we won't be getting back out again. We would have to stand or fall with the fortress."

Mia spoke up. "And you believe the fortress will fall?"

He nodded. "Landing at Cape Finngrath would make more sense. It's an easier march to Caldoness and Albaron's heartland. If they're landing on the treacherous shores here and making for the Redoubt, it's because they're coming for you both. Gregor and I were with Steward Kilkern when he received the first report of their advance. The scout wasn't optimistic about our chances of victory."

In spite of the sobering news, Mia was quick to reply, "Then we either stay and fight to hold a castle doomed to fall, or we proceed on foot over treacherous terrain with no supplies or escort?

"Surviving either would be a feat."

Silent tears gathered at the corners of Ilsa's cool blue eyes. Whether for herself, Mia, Lorelei, or them all was hard to say. Gregor gave a little bow and produced his kerchief. She took it with noticeable hesitance and a, "Thank you, Your Majesty," so low it was almost inaudible.

Releasing a weighty sigh, Mia added, "We would also be monsters to bring such suffering on these people while we have slipped away to save ourselves without a word."

Grimacing, Thomas felt the sting of truth cleansing the wound of deception that had been festering in him. Of course, they could not just abandon the Albarons to save themselves—and, as long as he was being honest with himself, to save Mia. Thus died his vain plans to secretly whisk her to safety. He took her hand gently.

Her hand tensed as if preparing to jerk away. Mia looked up at him and must have found something she needed in his expression. The iciness of earlier thawed by degrees. "We're staying," she confirmed.

He nodded.

"Then we had best hurry to get within the gates."

Giving her hand one more squeeze, he brought it up to his lips, brushed it with a tender kiss, and released it. Turning away from her, he marched up the path back to the Redoubt. That kiss on her hand may be the last of their lives. A maelstrom of feelings rose up, constricting his throat, but he pushed against it, struggling through the inward tumult. There was no time to face the implications of this choice, only to take the next steps ahead of them.

Halfway up the path, he noticed the gates to the fortress were opening again. Riders galloped out, led by Steward Kilkern himself. Thomas braced himself for a stern rebuke for muddling their defense with his disappearance and late return. There were more Albaron riders than he would expect for such a task. As they reached them, those behind the steward fanned out around them, encircling them.

Something is very wrong here.

As if hearing the thought, Steward Kilkern spoke up. "I see you found the Baroness."

"Yes." Thomas was somewhat confused by the harsh tone the steward employed and his seeming to forget it was he who told her to go see Lorelei in the Devastation tents. "She was right—"

The steward held up a hand. To the men flanking him, he addressed, "Take the Baroness an' her maiden to her quarters an' post a guard."

Four men did as instructed, so swiftly, and coarsely, Thomas could scarce react before they had both women by the wrists, dragging them back up the road. A little squeak of shock and incomprehension escaped Mia's lips as she struggled to face Thomas but was denied that chance.

Thomas's mouth hung open as he grappled with what to say. His hand drifted to the hilt of his spiritsword instinctively, resting there. "Your Honor, I'm still capable of defending—"

All around, the remaining mounted soldiers raised their spears and pointed them at Thomas, ensconcing him in a hedge of pointed steel tips. Thomas's grip tightened on his spiritsword. Some of the speartips drifted close enough he could wobble and nick his cheek on them.

Something is definitely wrong here.

"Steward Kilkern," Thomas began.

Over him, the steward instructed, "Keep the boy shackled in the hunting dogs' pen and take Sir Fenwrest down to the dungeons. The Monarch's forces will be here at dawn, an' we cannot lose the pinions of our bargain with him."

"*Pinions of his bargain ...*" Thomas muttered before it fully sank in. His sword was half drawn before he was nicked by a poignant jab reminding him not to be brash. Thomas scowled furiously at Steward Kilkern. Only a few hours ago, he had been lightly conversing with him. Thomas had admired him so thoroughly. "You've betrayed us!" he accused, though the tinge of question was impossible to remove from his words.

"Aye," the steward replied. He wheeled his horse around and rode off to the Redoubt as Thomas was slung to the ground. The path's rocky dust choked him as he was rudely stripped of his armaments and shackled. From where he lay, he could see they were doing the same to Gregor. He caught a glimpse of the terror in his younger cousin's eyes. In them, Thomas saw the death of not just themselves, but the Restoration and all the hope it carried.

7

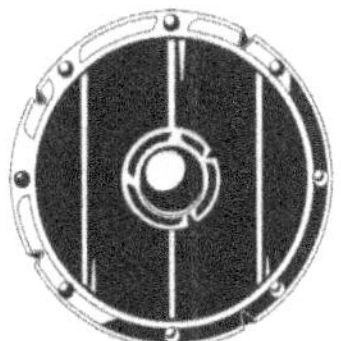

Thomas's jaw ached from the last blow he'd received for being impertinent. He'd lost count of how many he'd earned over his body since the betrayal and capture the night before. He managed to not lose his balance on the dank stairs winding up from the dungeon. The moss-slicked stones were more incongruous lumps on a natural slope than stonemason's craft. Prior stewards had made use of the dungeon such that the ominous tales of its dark depths had reached even Thomas's Ecthel ears as a young child. The suffering he had endured overnight felt all the more gross and cruel for knowing the present Steward masqueraded as a physician and caretaker of the vulnerable.

They reached the landing he remembered from the night before, and the wide wooden doors to beyond were jerked open after the appropriate knocked code. Pale dawn filtered in from distant windows and was as stark as a noon sun from his time in the dark depths. Even so, Thomas refused to wince or show any signs of discomfort. In the solitude, he'd sought the High King. Pleaded for aid. And he had felt some peace greet him in the interminable torment of impenetrable dark and damp that was the caverns of Kilkern dungeon.

One of the guards gave him a rough shove. He'd paused to luxuriate in the paltry warmth the early hour offered, which was much greater than the frigid dungeon.

The blow aggravated other injuries incurred, those without, those within. Thomas buried the pain deep beneath the layers of stone he'd laid since the sting of the Steward's treachery first beset him. Within his heart warred the pain and fear and anger and sorrow. A vicious brawl like the famed gladiatorial spectacles of Tislatna. The stone-like dome he cast over it all was keeping him from being rent to pieces. He would not give Steward Kilkern nor the Monarch the satisfaction of seeing him broken by their machinations.

Another large set of doors were opened before them, and they entered the main audience chamber for the castle from its left wing. On a dais, seated on the throne known as the Second Seat—the First being the High King's throne in the Highland— was the Steward. His gaze flicked to Thomas and lingered only an instant before turning back to the front of the room.

Thomas spotted Gregor, muddied and hunched over. The boy looked as awful as Thomas felt, and for that, the teen doubly begrudged Steward Kilkern. Death would be too good an end for such a traitor, so Thomas instead let his imagination rest first on torments fitting for such malignancy and disloyalty. At least for a moment, until bile rose in his throat and he thought he might choke on the fantasies. Such retribution was forbidden to a Knight. It was not the manner of the Order or sanctioned by the High King. Shame was something new to keep in the vault of anguish he was constructing around his heart.

There was little time to dwell on it. Across the room, the large ceremonial doors creaked open. A luxurious red carpet made from some finer fabric other than the rough spun wool typically produced in the region ran from the dais to the entrance of the room. Thomas noted the bits of golden finery around the chamber and felt disgusted that such niceties were in the possession of such an odious man to celebrate the arrival of one still more foul.

With the doors fully opened, a party garbed in the black and green of the Monarch's soldiers marched in with ceremonial precision. Two lines formed on either side of the carpet, weapons held in a salute of sorts. Thomas craned a bit to see. Loathsome as he was, Thomas had never seen Monarch Ilyron before and was curious about him. Until he was smacked backward by one of his guards. He needn't have worked so hard. Several moments later, a figure emerged from the midst of the lined soldiers, a smaller escort flanking either side. And it wasn't the mysterious Monarch. It was someone else he recognized.

"Hale morning, Lady Delia Sornfold of Emeral," Steward Kilkern called out and stood. "Kilkern's Redoubt welcomes you warmly."

"Steward Kilkern, we accept your gracious welcome, with but two contentions. I am styled as Queen Delia Ilyron of Ecthelowall," she replied, a smile playing on her maroon-colored lips. They matched her dress which was tightly fitted in the bodice and flared out in mounds of luxuriant silky fabric. All of it was etched with bands of dark green fabric bearing gleaming streaks which may have been real gold woven in. Delia's pallid skin and flaxen hair were the same as Thomas remembered. Any man in the Lowlands not privy to the content of her heart would find her beautiful. But he knew she was more than a rose with thorns, she was belladonna. Deceptive in her outward comeliness and deadly.

It was difficult not to notice the tiara she wore as well. A radiate crown, golden and sharply pointed. "And second, I can't help but note you have not extended the same courtesy to the little pig the Restoration calls its *Heir Apparent*." Her smile broadened.

Kilkern was more guarded in his expressions. Perhaps understanding the danger of the woman before him. "I had hoped to please the Monarch himself with the display. I can't help but note he has not come himself as agreed upon."

Delia's smile remained warm, inviting, as if she were laughing while on a romp in a field under the summer sun. "Your lord is detained at the moment. He is currently securing an expansion in the accord with the Vogteremark."

"Do tell."

Without her pleased expression slipping for a moment, Delia replied, "I will not. You will be accorded any counsel you need as it becomes necessary. My husband needs not comport his dealings to Albaron vassals."

There was a narrowing around Kilkern's eyes. "I suppose my congratulations on your marriage are in order. My gift to you both is a word of wisdom. In Albaron, the Stewards exist as a parliament of equals. Our duty is to our people and lands first, the Laird having no claim other than our universal consent to be one people. Your husband will do well to remember that if he intends to draw the other Stewards from the war and into *vassalage*. Albaron may not be able to win a war with him, but we can certainly leave a wound that will ensure he will be in no condition to fight any others."

Like the first frost of the season, Delia's tone abruptly chilled, even though her expression was still convivial. "You are over pert, *steward*. Fortunately for you, your lord and lady appreciate a bit of verve."

Her eyes drifted and fell on Thomas. They brightened in recognition and soon after, a despicable pleasure. "You have captured both Fenwrest boys! You did not send word you had nabbed both troublemakers. Our spies tell us Thomas is now my sister's personal bodyguard. That cannot be true, though, because I do not see her among the guests here today."

"Your spies' insights are keen and right," Kilkern admitted. "Though your couriers and courtiers seem lacking. The Monarch himself approved of my keeping her in cloister under my watch."

For just a moment, Thomas's heart beat wild against the confines he'd placed around it, hope pressing against the barriers to hold in the sorrow and pain. Mia was to escape death!

Delia's expression finally slipped from its dimensions of put-upon pleasantness. "You were married once, weren't you, steward?"

Kilkern's façade slipped, and beneath his tight reply was an edge, "Yes. She passed on, er, not many months ago."

The Steward had not revealed that to Thomas. From the way Delia had spoken she was well aware he had been wedded, and likely as not, the nature and cause of the Stewardess consort's death. Could it have had something to do with why the Steward was betraying the Restoration?

Some of the smile Delia wore returned. "Then I'm sure you'll remember that a man's word is only as good as his wife agrees it to be?"

Taking a purposeful step forward, Kilkern was hard as the stone of the Redoubt. "That is not our way in Albaron. A man and his wife are lovers and mates here, with no time for such childish plays at power and control."

Once more, Delia managed to craft whatever ire she felt into barbs for her words instead of letting it weigh down her smile. "Perhaps you should also consider then, that I'm not just the Queen consort of Ecthelowall. I'm also the crowned

Princess of Emeral, and my sister has assumed the title Baroness of Yerst and Emeral.

"Once word of your treachery spreads, should any of your fellow Stewards not see your wisdom in submitting to the Monarch, they will come for you. My army will be all that stands between you and your warrior brothers obliterating you."

Glowering at Delia, Kilkern bit out, "Very well." To one of the guards near him, he gestured and instructed, "Go retrieve Lady Sornfold."

"And her maiden," Delia amended.

The steward's brows knitted. At length, he added heavily, "Bring them both here in irons. Immediately."

The guard nodded and left to retrieve Mia, and with his departure, any ghost of the hope Thomas had allowed to swell the space guarding his heart. He could feel Delia's gaze on him as much as he saw it. It was all he could do to not show forth any more despair than would be fitting for one whose task was to defend Mia. Thomas was certain if she knew he loved her sister, then she would find myriads of ways to intensify her cruelty to the both of them.

Agonizingly, the time passed until the guard towed Mia and Ilsa into view, each shackled at the wrist with irons, as instructed. Neither looked bruised or battered, however, and Mia was dressed in her most regal emerald gown. Tenacity burned in her eyes of the same green, and it did his heart good to see her so defiant. Ilsa was demure, but alert, taking in the scene of the court. When her eyes lighted on Gregor, she seemed to wince.

"Hello, sister," Delia crowed. "You have been busy since you slipped away from Emeral."

At that moment, seeing the wicked turn of Delia's maroon lips, Thomas knew it didn't matter whether Delia knew about

Mia and his love or not. Whatever darkness had twisted her heart from the young woman he had known as a child now ensured that she would be monstrously cruel to them both without cause or goading. Which would mean not just seeing Mia die, but watching her slowly slip away from him in agony.

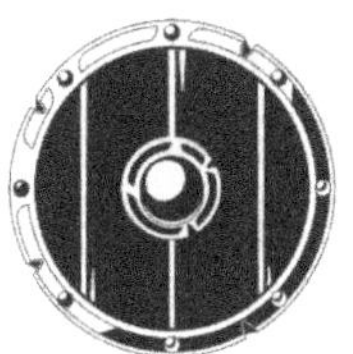

"You are right, sister," Mia almost spat the last word. "I have been busy. Busy aiding the cause that most honors our ancestors."

Delia gave a derisive snort. "Ha. Honored that boor of a father we shared, you mean? Or have you forgotten that you fled the island after our people rose up in support of me?"

"Not everyone on Emeral is bewitched by you. Soon, very soon, those loyal to the true Emeral and justice will rise up and expel your poison from our land!" Mia made no attempt at masking her contempt or anger.

This was news to Thomas. Had Mia been secretly communicating with someone on Emeral? If so, why not tell him? Besides the fact that he would've advised against such a risky move. Whomever she had consorted with could easily be the traitor who divulged that they were presently at Kilkern's Redoubt.

"A pity you will not live to see your pathetic attempt to rebel come to pass. As the rightful Princess of our homeland and Queen consort of the Monarchy of Ecthelowall, I can order my loyal vassal, the Steward, to cut you down where you stand …"

Mia's eyes shot to the Steward. During her confinement, she must have figured out that he had betrayed them to the Monarch. But the depth and substance of that betrayal, that he chose to become a servant of evil instead of merely skirting confrontation with it, visibly shook her.

Delia giggled with delight. "However, I have something more fitting in mind." Cocking her head to the side, she regarded Mia for a moment longer before saying. "Perhaps an example still needs made. Bring forward her attendant."

As the guards grabbed Ilsa, she went rigid. Her eyes fixed to the distance as if in a trance. The Albarons dragged her over to stand before Delia. Thomas strained against those holding him back. Not Ilsa. Not Ilsa who, despite her sturdy Dag Votere build, was meek and modest as a violet. Not Ilsa, who would never harm a mouse, much less a man. And most of all not dear Ilsa, who he, while outside Mia's chambers on guard, could hear singing childhood lullabies to Mia to help her sleep easier.

"*No!* She's just a servant!" he cried out.

"Quiet you," hissed one of those holding him back and delivered Thomas a sharp punch to his side that dropped him to his knees. The guards at either side of him jerked his arms back so far that they felt like they were being ripped out of their sockets.

Once again, Delia was the she viper, taking in his futile pleas for mercy. Her regard was as if she tasted the air with her forked tongue to determine if love or lust had made him speak up. Those could be powerful tools of torment if true. How she could tell the difference, Thomas wasn't sure. But she must have realized his outburst was born of compassion rather than the others because back to her prey she returned. Drawing a dagger, she held the little blade up and commented, "This is the same dagger I used on Father. The poison on it is excruciating, torturous. Once I've finished with your maiden, little sister, this is what you may look forward to."

"You beast!" Gregor shouted, his voice choked with emotion and the pain of injuries he had received since the day prior. "Have you no sense of justice at all? Or has the Monarch stolen it away with whatever worth to this world you once had?"

Turning to face the boy, Thomas could not see Delia's expression. Only her precise, menacing movements that made it seem like she was coiling to strike. "'Whatever worth I once had?' How dare you, of all people, say such a thing, you little swine! You the filthy, foolish child to whom my father would have sold me into bondage. What sense of justice could a pig like you presume to hold over anyone?

"If the Monarch did not wish to see you before you die, I would carve you and roast you here and now!"

Delia whirled back around toward Ilsa, who was still vacant in her expression. It was almost as though she was under a spell. Drawing herself up into a regal posturing, Delia announced, "This is what awaits all who defy me."

Quick as a serpent's strike, Delia drew back and plunged the dagger forward. Thomas closed his eyes and winced as he heard Ilsa suck in a sharp breath and gasp.

9

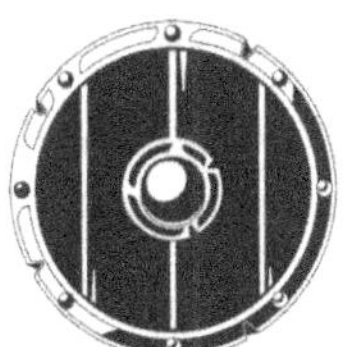

Behind the closed lids of his eyes, Thomas saw nothing but heard a rush as of wind. An icy rush of air hit him an instant before a retaliatory surge of heat pushed back against it. Warmth coursed along his frame and he luxuriated in the sensation. His eyes blinked open and he could see the room as it had been before, but to his shock, his guards were no longer holding him in place.

The disturbance, the rush of air and the warmth following it—those could only have been the touch of the High King, couldn't they? Certainly, it would explain what else he saw. Ilsa seemed to shimmer, her hair golden and her face aglow with awe. One hand, no longer bound, reached toward her bosom as if her breath had been stolen away. A wide smile of wonder parted her lips.

In stark contrast, Delia recoiled, her face a twisted snarl ready to launch a hundred black curses. Her usual fair complexion seemed ashen, and her hair stringy and sooty. All her pronounced curves which caught the eye of every man who saw her shrank and sagged as if she had been greatly aged.

Most startling was the black around her eyes. As though the inverse of a lighthouse, they removed light from around them instead of shining it abroad. Markings on her skin that had been hidden began glowing. Drawing attention to the dagger she had been in the act of plunging into Ilsa's abdomen—or rather its total absence. A fact not lost on Delia, by all appearances.

She slung the charred remains of her weapon onto the stone with a clatter. A screech and growl in one loosed from her lips, "Phosphila—little light lover—Ilyron warned me of your kind!"

For a moment Ilsa seemed at a loss and then, her eyes swept the room and she very quietly murmured, "And I have been warned of yours since childhood. You have become a Tislatnean witch!"

"I have become more than you can understand," Delia replied with a deepening menace as the chamber's ambiance returned to normal. It seemed as if the shadows of the room were drawn to Delia, and under their care, her appearance was restored to the remarkable beauty she'd always possessed.

"Is it true, Delia?" Thomas whispered under his breath.

One smoothly arched eyebrow raised, and Delia's full maroon lips twisted up into a satisfied smirk as though she heard Thomas's question and was amused by it.

"Ahem." The Steward cleared his throat. "This has all been very ... amusing, but perhaps it would be best to send the prisoners back to confinement for the present. We have prepared a feast in Your Honor in addition to some traditional Albaron games for more conventional entertainment."

The smirk blossomed into a condescending smile. "While watching your men fall over themselves in the folly you Albarons call sport sounds delightful, I will be taking the prisoners and departing. Immediately. I have pressing business in Wyvares."

The stiffening in Steward Kilkern's posture was pronounced. "Wyvares? My lady, no one has seen Wyvares in centuries. If it ever existed. It is a place we tell our children of in stories to send shivers down their shanks. What fool has set you on such an errand?"

"My husband, your Monarch," she replied, dryly. "His army shall be meeting mine there as soon as he dispatches the garrison at Dirkforge."

"Legends always speak of Wyvares being situated in the frigid north, the Upper Albar Mountains. That's a far jaunt from Dirkforge." The tightness in Steward Kilkern's voice was undeniable. Something about this Wyvares, which Thomas had never heard of, thoroughly unsettled the otherwise stoic man. Was it genuine fear of kinder tales, or was it the brazen declaration that the Monarchists could move so freely through the Albaron heartland even as it gave its full measure of effort to drive the Ecthels back?

If the latter, it was understandable. Nearly all of Albaron's defenses were aimed at discouraging any Ecthel incursions into their territory. Particularly from the Annàmhaid Sea. However, were his unease to purely originate from the naming of Wyvares, Thomas was at a loss as to what could so frighten this man of science, who did not even fear to betray and beat servants of the High King of All Realms.

"If that is your manner of offering your services as a loyal retainer, then I shall pass your interest to the Monarch. If it is idle curiosity about the affairs of war, tread carefully Steward."

Delia said the last with such sharpness that it could have cut every cerulean tapestry from the walls of the room. For his part, Kilkern took the implicit rebuke in stride. "Then, my lady, we shall send you on your way with full hearts and our humble gratitude for your visit."

Standing, Steward Kilkern raised his arm in an Albaron

gesture of honor and respect. If Delia was aware of its significance, she did not show it, merely returning a nod. It seemed, in fact, that she had no interest whatsoever left in the Steward. She spun on her heels and called to her guards, swathed in the deep green and black of the Monarchists, their silvery helms and halberds gleaming even in the soft candle lighting of the room. "Take each of them under custody and ensure they remain separate." She glanced over her shoulder at Thomas, her eyes narrowed and her lips pursed. To her soldiers she added, "And there is no need to treat them kindly. Be as rough as you like with all of them."

10

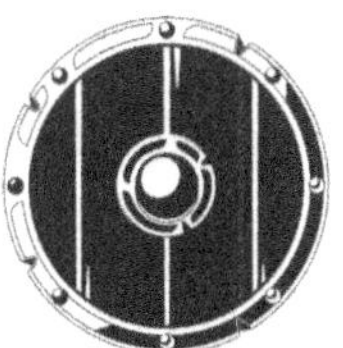

It was a brutal march out and away from Kilkern's Redoubt, heading north and east. Skirting the space between the Eigh River and Treigl Mountains, the local arm of the Albar Mountains, the pace kept was not one Thomas would expect of an army guarding a Queen consort. Heady with slick rocks that sloped down into a river valley, this was no terrain for rushing. Yet, at times, they almost ran, never a word spoken among any of the Monarchists as to why they hurried so. As night fell on the first day of their travels and they finally set up camp, the only thing Thomas could guess that pushed them on was whatever lay in wait at their alleged destination, Wyvares.

As soon as a camp was set, Thomas was shackled to the primary support pole of a dark tent and left alone. There he sat, watching as the interior of his confinements dimmed with the setting sun. He tried not to let his thoughts become equally dark. It was a struggle. Mia and Gregor were held by Delia, who was more than just an ally of the Monarch, she had been twisted into something truly dark. Her ease with ending life was so evil that Thomas couldn't reconcile it with the sun-kissed girl he remembered. The one who used to gather flowers in the meadows outside Yerst Castle and gaze off into the distance as if she walked the marches of Ecthelowall and those of dreams at the same time. He could not remember a single scowl, a single harsh word from her. Not until her first love, Mark, died. But even then, she was only silent, distant. She had stopped collecting flowers, but Thomas took that to be her growing older, maturing into the *important* role Commonwealth society had for her. When did her smiles become sinister?

It didn't matter, ultimately, but he couldn't make it not matter to him. Maybe he felt he owed it to his cousin Mark to find that point of inflection in Delia. Maybe in finding it, he could help pull her back to the light. More likely, his heart insisted on it because of Mia. Her sister had been manipulated and used by their father as a tool for his advancement. Perhaps, in time, Mia could forgive Delia's hatred and murder of their father. But not this Delia. This monster.

Thomas's chest ached at what Mia must be enduring right now. Physical tortures aside, Delia was the last of her family left, and this was worse than if Delia had simply died. Then she could have been mourned and eulogized and remembered, if bittersweetly. What Mia had to endure was the ravaging of every warm, glowing memory between them. Every moment of her life past marred by all that Delia was doing and would do if not stopped.

If Delia isn't stopped, Mia won't have long to suffer.

No, he couldn't let that thought find a home in his heart or mind. Mia wasn't going to die. If he had to break both his hands and fight through every soldier in this camp, that could not happen. He would ... he would ...

A wave of despair crashed over him as he tugged futilely at his restraints. He wasn't rescuing anyone like this. Why couldn't he be as strong and wise as Cinaed of Tislatna? A true hero. Or even as much so as his fellow Knights, Terrillian and Anargen? They were only a few years older, yet they had done incredible things.

With the High King's aid ...

My King, how can you allow this to stand? Why have you left me here to watch helplessly as everyone I love in the Lowlands dies around me? Don't you care?

There was silence. The words were bitter, biting within him. Lashing his heart further.

Why was it others succeeded where he had so miserably failed? The whole of Ecthelowall had been depending on him to fulfill his duty to keep Mia and Gregor safe. Was it because they were Ecthels? Did the High King intend for Ecthelowall to destroy itself?

Quick, purposeful footsteps sounded on the stoney ground outside. The tent fabric rustled as it was swept aside, and two Monarchist soldiers stalked in, each grabbing Thomas brusquely under the arms and pinning them back. A third, who had held the flap, stalked in and undid the chain holding Thomas to the tent pole. "Her Highness has requested we fetch you. Do yourself a favor and keep your mouth shut."

"No prom—" a swift backhand from the guard cut Thomas off and left his mouth with the unpleasant taste of blood.

"Mouth shut," the soldier reiterated. Eyeing Thomas until the teen had the good sense to look down in deference, the soldier nodded to the other two, who hauled Thomas out of the tent and through the sprawling camp. Fires denoting companies of soldiers dotted the valley. If Thomas had to guess, there were at least four hundred men. A large contingent to sneak about with, but hardly enough to take any of the seven major castle cities of Albaron.

Well, any of the six others that didn't turn traitorous.

Overhead, the indigo expanse of night was clouded over. Only the palest diffusion of that steely dome of cloud cover hinted that beyond shone a bright moon, near full, eager to offer its light, but shut out. Thomas kept his eye on that mottled patch of the sky until the moment he was shoved into a large tent curtained off into multiple rooms. An unnecessarily rough push sent him to the ground inside the largest of the tent's enclosures. He was slugged for his lapse in balance and then forced up to face Delia. She was clad now in a softer, silkier gown of the evening that hugged her bodice more closely. Something that would no doubt have enticed most men of the Lowlands, but it only galled Thomas to see her so at ease and comfortable, knowing Mia was no doubt suffering somewhere close.

Another group of soldiers clomped in and threw down Ilsa next to Thomas. They held them both firmly in place.

Delia stood, her lips parting in a smile that radiated warmth and congeniality. "Ah, thank you, Sergeant. You may wait outside. I will call for you if needed."

"Your Highness," he replied, sounding hesitant. He eyed Thomas and his bonds before giving a bow to her and exiting the tent.

As soon as he was gone, Delia took a small stick and went to some brass censers hung around the tent and lit the contents within. A heavy press of a sickly sweet scent rolled over Thomas. He tried to not gag and have his last bit of dignity robbed. He struggled with success but couldn't help coughing once the smoke from the incense filled the space.

"My apologies," Delia said as she reclaimed her seat on a luxurious sedan they must be transporting for her. "Albaron is a starkly beautiful country but smells wretched. Particularly when we make such hasty encampment as this. Is it too much for you?"

Thomas didn't say anything. There had been a genuine note of concern in her voice. Was he imagining all of this? Hadn't Delia been vicious enough to rip his throat out if provoked at Kilkern's Redoubt?

As if sensing his thoughts, she held up a hand imploring. "Please, take ease, each of you. We have much to discuss."

"Like how you plan to kill us?" Thomas retorted, shooting Ilsa a look assessing her well-being. She seemed largely unharmed. Her hair was even braided into a long silvery tail. Ilsa kept her blue eyes fixed forward.

"My apologies to you both. You no doubt refer to that bit of theatrics I was forced to employ in the Steward's audience chamber. I had to appear ruthless and strong for the crude men of Albaron. They see a young, courtly woman such as I and think me something to be used. I could not allow that.

"You see my vision for the Monarchy of Ecthelowall is far more magnanimous and compassionate than you may suspect. One in which every subject is well-fed and kept safe. Where thoughts and aspirations and beauty may flourish. That's why I brought you both to me. I know the men disabused you, and I would not want you to have the misimpression that such represents the Ecthelowall that can be. The one I'm devoting myself to crafting once this horrid war is ended."

It may have been the haze in the room playing tricks on him, or the lethargy and fogginess of mind he felt now, but Thomas wondered again after how sincere she sounded. It was so jarring and so much more like the Delia he remembered from childhood.

"Of course, Your Highness," Ilsa replied. "Speak on." This time Ilsa shot Thomas a look, her brows furrowed and her posturing wobbling as though her thoughts were becoming muddled.

"I've brought you both before me to offer you a great benevolence."

"Great benevolence?" Ilsa asked, her voice hopeful.

Deep within, Thomas felt a stabbing pang of concern. Concern that what he had witnessed in the Steward Kilkern's Hall was indeed an act by the High King on her behalf. That she, too, had pledged herself to him. But her eagerness to hear the spider croon to its captured flies was troubling.

Or maybe it isn't. Maybe I misjudged Delia.

The thought was ephemeral and in and out of his mind with no residue. A vapor drifting past him. But how and where did it come from?

"Yes, very great," Delia confirmed, her voice silken as a strand of web. "I offer each of you a chance to change your fate. In the present social ordering, you each are expendables. More important than commoners, but not as free in your choices each day either."

The haze from the censers had taken on a green tinge. Little green tendrils twisted like slithering serpents through the air. Delia breathed in deeply, seemingly pleased with the aroma of her incense. She held out her hand to Thomas as if offering him a gift, tendrils of the smoke twisted around it and arced outward towards him. "You endured a great tragedy that robbed you of your birthright. What if I told you, you could have your father's lands and title restored to you?"

It took a moment for the words to reach him as if they were echoes from a great distance. "But that can't happen. My uncle holds those claims."

Delia arched an eyebrow, stirring her finger in the spreading mists. "You mean the uncle who has rebelled against his Monarch? The Isle of Fens will need a new Baron, along with Langlan's Bay and its surrounding lands. Both could be accorded to you."

"I—" Thomas began to protest but found it hard to form his argument. Was he, by habit, silent before his betters? If so, it only made what Delia offered infuriatingly alluring. Part of him balked at the offer, but part whispered a reminder that if the title was his, he could court any woman he chose.

Mia.

But no ... how ... Delia is going to kill Mia.

More of the incense cloud spread. Delia's hand swept dramatically in offering to Ilsa. "You, Ilsa Gavmild, could become so much more than a handmaid of a usurper. You are foreign born, Dag Vogtere by ancestry, yes?"

Ilsa nodded, her eyes wide, fixated on Delia. "Yes, my lady."

"Soon, new lands here in Albaron and Libertias will be added to Ecthelowall's domain. We will need capable rulers of these marches. You, too, could ascend and become a Baroness to be served rather than serve."

There was something berry-sweet, oversweet, about Delia's tone and demeanor. It matched the incense's odor. She had always possessed charm, and her beauty only made her effect on others more potent. This was different. It set Thomas's hairs on end, because the more he tried to question and turn back from embracing the offers, the more they felt like commands. These compulsions exerted a pull like gravity, dragging them swiftly down into Delia's will. It was more than being hemmed in by the words, it felt as if his wits were being walled in, sequestered without release.

How is she doing it?

Delia's dark lips parted in pleasure. "You are both speechless. I did tell you it was great benevolence!

"I ask one thing in return. You must tell me where Viceroy Ecthelion is presently." Then her eyes narrowed with sinister glee. "Oh, but I'm a forgetful one. I must confess there is a further stipulation. Only one of you need tell me this information. So, of course, only one of you may receive the reward. Which of you will act first to transcend your fate and claim what you deserve, I wonder?"

Thomas looked at Ilsa and saw her eyes bright, conflicted. She pursed her lips as if in great concentration. Was she about to give in?

No. Resisting. She's resisting, like me.

The thoughts were barely Thomas's own for the haze he had to get through to find them. They were lights, beamed to him from beyond his murky captivity. Echoing within those mists of his mind were Delia's words, "Only one ... Only one ..."

"Only one ..." Thomas repeated, struggling.

Delia all but cackled with delight. "Of course, dear Thomas. That's very good. Poor boy, you've lost so much. Will you be the one?"

"No," he said. Thomas shook his head as if to dispel the unseen fog. "I can't be the one. Gregor ..."

"The little pig will be dead soon," Delia crooned.

That sharpened Thomas's focus. The thought of harm to Gregor was like a waypoint, he could use to find his way out. "If I ... take his place ... then ... I would be a rival."

"A rival?" Delia repeated, consternation furrowing her brow for an instant. She didn't look pleased he'd had the thought, and she stirred the literal mists from her incense burners again.

"Yes ... Ilyron's. I would be his rival ... if my title ... was restored."

For a moment Delia stopped wafting the incense and crinkled her nose. "Hmm, perhaps. All the more reason for you to take my offer with haste."

Thomas's brows furrowed in confusion as much as

concentration. "You would accept ... a challenge ... to your husband's rule?"

She snorted. "If a deign to, silly boy."

"What sort ... of love ... is that?"

"Love?" Delia's tone grew heated. "What is love but a spirit by which to drunken fools?"

Thomas's thoughts were no longer so fogbound. "How can you ... say that ... after Mark?"

Delia's countenance darkened, fierce as a fresh summer storm. "He is why I know love is a pretty game we play to keep each other shackled. Weak and worthless."

Why did Delia's views on love matter to him? Once more the specter of Mia and all the harm to her heart such cruelty from her sister would inflict presented itself. Though something more seemed beyond that, something that whispered to him in this dark hour. And so, he fought. "Love is more than you realize. It's greater than what enables the moving of mountains at a word. It's greater than what allows a man to stand in wait for the promise of millennia not yet fulfilled."

"What poetic nonsense," Delia retorted. Sneering as if sniffing a repugnant miasma wafting among her incense. "Love didn't save Mark. It didn't rescue me from my father's schemes. And it certainly isn't helping you now."

"That's where you're wrong," Thomas replied, feeling the walls hemming his mind in giving under his pressure. In its crumbling he had a clear view beyond to what drove him forward. To the source of the light beyond the mists, which he was now certain was an enchantment Delia had somehow worked. The source of all light guided him free. Every inch of him rippled with warmth, the divine fire that, if his spiritsword were but in hand, could incinerate this entire camp. But it wasn't in hand, and he looked to Ilsa, knowing that if he spoke what burned in his heart it would no doubt mean harm to them both.

Her eyes, hazy at first, seemed to clear the longer they lingered on him. Shaking her head, Ilsa seemed to have escaped the fog herself. A slight nod was all the approval she gave. It was enough, and he decided he had been right about the burst of light and fire days before. Delia may torment them, but she could scarce hope to break one Knight of Light, much less two supporting each other.

"Patient. Kind. Forgiving," he began, his voice resonating like an invocation. "Love is all that, and more. It rejoices with the truth. It bears all things. Believes all things. Your power over me is temporary, but love never ends."

Little cinders danced in the air around them as the incense cloud burned away. In the over-sweet smell's absence were heavy, more discordant odors. It was exhilarating and puzzling in one. Could the High King's fire work when the words were merely spoken instead of inscribed on a spiritsword?

"Ugh, how did you ..." Delia bristled and then her eyes narrowed on Ilsa. "Ah, I should have seen this sooner. You have an enchantress yourself. One who seems to have put her spell upon you."

For a moment, Thomas was confused. As he watched Delia slink slowly toward Ilsa, like a predator a strange new source of potential prey, he realized it.

Delia thinks Ilsa has been behind everything. The fire that destroyed the dagger, my words, and breaking whatever spell they were under!

He wanted to cry out to contradict her, but what good would it do? Delia would only think him a love-sickened pawn of a witch. Watching in horror Delia raised her gloved hand and withdrew its dark velvety fabric. The hand that had held the dagger before. It looked as gaunt and diseased as the day before, as if it had never recovered its facade.

"Ilyron warned me that dark magic sometimes has a heavy price," she began. "But he has also shown me its potent rewards. If I drain it from whatever talisman you possess, little Ilsa, imagine what wonders I could achieve ..."

She reached for Ilsa's throat as if to choke her. Thomas couldn't stand still a moment longer. Throwing himself, bound, he barreled into Delia, sending her tumbling into the side of the tent where cases of supplies were stacked. Instead of there being a crash and Delia landing sprawled on the ground, he watched her body melt into a black stain that zipped behind him, nothing but a shadow on the tent's floor.

What in the Lowlands?

His head snapped around as he heard a hissed whisper, "Such devotion. Looks like you're as much a fool as the rest of the Fenwrest boys."

Somehow, impossibly, Delia was there, standing behind him.

No, not impossible. He had been told of something similar. Anargen had spoken of mystic assassins who could merge with the shadows at a whim. "Sombra," he murmured as if in accusation.

Delia smirked triumphantly. "Oh, I'm far more than that." But her eyes were sharply fixed on Ilsa. "Far, far more."

She took another step toward Ilsa, and sharp notes of some kind echoed in from the valley without. Once, twice, a third time the strident calls of a ram's horn battered their way into the tent. For a moment, Thomas's heart swelled against the bounds he had placed around it, the chamber he forced it to reside in to keep pain and despair from eviscerating him.

That's a battle summons for Albaron's armies.

An instant later, one of the Monarchists tore open the tent flap and stumbled in. "Your Highness, we are under attack!"

11

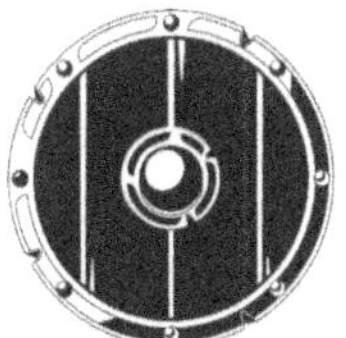

More than anything, Delia looked annoyed. "We were well hidden here. Any forces from Caldoness or southward should have taken days to cross the mountains."

The messenger just stood there, looking like a scolded pup. When he failed to speak, Delia sighed. "Under attack by whom? How many do they bring? Speak up, Sergeant."

"The Albarons, Your Highness. They have hundreds."

"Foolhardy Albarons," Delia cursed. "How long till they're upon us?"

The messenger trembled and gestured emphatically, "They're already upon us. We must get you to safety!"

Delia's eyes narrowed on the short stocky man, who wasn't much more than a boy. "You men of Ecthelowall are all the same. Useless and feckless. Prepare my litter and guard to travel. I will drive these pests back into their dens."

She moved in long swift strides toward the tent's entrance and paused halfway there. Glancing back at Thomas and Ilsa, she struck the Sergeant on his shoulder. "Dispose of him along

65

with that little pig, Gregor. This handmaid is to be brought along. Understood?"

"Yes, Your Highness." He gave her a military salute.

She rolled her icy eyes and then pinned Thomas down with a stare. "It looks like this will be goodbye. Try not to scream too much when they kill you. It's what Mark would have wanted, after all," she mocked and then disappeared out into the night.

A chill cut through the air of the tent, and Thomas wondered what Delia could possibly do against an army. Not just an army, an army of Albarons. It was possible the Albarons were here to rescue Mia and Gregor, but more likely scouts had seen the Monarchist group's movements and were dispatched to drive them back or destroy them. So, whether Delia could make good on her threat to deal with them or not, Thomas had to act now or never.

From the halting way he moved, the young Sergeant hadn't overcome his shock at his newly crowned Queen marching out unarmed against an army. But Thomas had, and as the Sergeant's eyes fell on Thomas, he lowered his shoulder and exploded into the Sergeant.

"Oof!" the young man cried as Thomas drove him backward into a tent pole.

Thomas's shoulder ached with the jarring impact of his bruised flesh against the Sergeant's steel cuirass, but he gritted through it. Pivoting back, he leaped forward in a headbutt that connected with the other man's face as he slid down the pole.

The stunned Sergeant hit his head on the pole and slumped to the ground, unconscious.

Thomas took in a steadying breath as he waited for the spots to fade from his vision. It was a more brutal attack than he could approve of, but he was low on options and even shorter on time. He shot a glance to check on Ilsa and found her eyeing him with furrowed brows. Her assessment of what had happened was inscrutable. Dropping to the ground beside the Sergeant, he rummaged for the keys to their bonds. Finding them, he fumbled to use them on his shackles. Once freed, he stood and walked over to Ilsa.

She took a step back, eyeing him warily.

"It's okay," he assured her, holding up the keys for her to see. "I'm going to undo your bonds."

"My bonds," she repeated as though just becoming aware of their existence again. "Of course. Thank you."

He undid the lock, and the restraints clanked to the ground. Ilsa rubbed her wrists where they had been shackled. "That was quite something. Did you learn that from a Knight of Light?"

"Ah, yes and no," he admitted. "My mentor and predecessor, Sir Hurstwell, taught me that. But he wasn't able to impart much of his wisdom as a Knight before his passing. Or at least I wasn't listening well enough till it was too late."

"He died on the Isle of Geists?" Ilsa recalled tentatively.

"Yes." Thomas drew in a sharp breath. "He sacrificed his life to save Mia, Gregor, and I from ..." he hesitated for a moment. For some reason, he felt ill at ease disclosing the details of the battle with the goblin that ultimately cost Hurstwell his life. Though he started to push the words into his mouth multiple times, they were struck down before ever passing through the doors of lips. Peculiar.

"A monster," he was able to finish at last. "But I can speak more of him another time. We must get to Gregor and Mia and set them free. This attack is just what we need to escape."

"Leave the Baroness to me," Ilsa suggested. "You should focus on getting Gregor."

Thomas shook his head. "No, we need to stick together. If they catch either of us, the guards would no doubt use the captured one as leverage to halt the escape attempt."

"And you plan to headbutt your way through the remaining guards?" she quipped, a sarcastic edge he had never heard from her before heavy in her tone.

He scowled. "No. I'm going to get back my spiritsword first."

"Hmph. And how do you hope to find it in all this camp, in the dark, while a battle rages around you?" Peering out the tent flaps, he motioned to Ilsa to follow. Just before racing out, he whispered, "It's hard to describe, but I just feel sure it's near."

It felt so close, in fact, that as soon as he peeked out of the tent, he shuffled toward another about ten feet away. There were no other soldiers to stop him. All of them—whatever Delia's boasting about handling matters herself—were pulled into the battle. Thomas could see it raging a hundred yards to what he believed was the south. Flaming arrows and torches made monstrous the sounds of steel clanging against steel and men and horses crying out in pain and fury.

Within the tent he was drawn to were packs and crates of supplies. On top of a long pine box lay the spiritsword he'd been given by Sir Terrillian. Without hesitation, he ran in and laid hold of it. The warmth and heat of the flames that rose up the blade's length were so welcome on this chilly night. Its light was an even greater comfort.

Nearby, he saw that his armor had also been tossed into a crate as if it were common hearth wares. With great care, he took each piece of armor and put it on, feeling more and more complete as he did. Once finished, it occurred to him that he needed to find Gregor's spiritsword.

From at his back, he heard Ilsa call, "You've found your

sword and more! Wonderful. If we hurry now, I think we might slip away unnoticed."

Facing her for an instant, he nodded. "Just a moment. I have to find Gregor's spiritsword."

"But his honor is not a Knight," she countered.

Surprised to hear her protest, Thomas hesitated. It felt as if he most certainly needed to retrieve the spiritsword. "It was Sir Hurstwell's," he began. "It may not yet burn for Gregor, but I know it will someday, and he would sorely regret losing it."

"As much as he would regret losing his life? Or ours?"

Gnawing on his lower lip, Thomas turned away from his fruitless scanning of the tent. Ilsa did make a point. Was his judgment clouded by the sword's sentimental value?

"I would imagine not," Thomas admitted. "Freeing Gregor and Mia is the priority."

"Come with me," Ilsa said, her voice filled with sympathy. "I think I saw where they're keeping Mia on my way to Queen Delia's tent."

"Then lead on." Thomas dashed over to Ilsa's side.

Ilsa did just that without another word, taking them both on a winding trek through tents as the sounds of the battle beyond grew closer. The Monarchist line was faltering and would give soon. They had to hurry.

Coming upon a rather small and unassuming tent, Ilsa held back the tent flap and nodded for Thomas to enter first. Leaping inside, he bared his spiritsword. There were no guards in this tent either, but a dark shape in the corner of the tent stirred. Thomas's eyes adjusted to the burning blade's luminance in the tight space. By it, he could make out Mia's form, partly sprawled on the ground, partly braced against a support pole. Her back was to him, and he saw her stiffen and straighten when his armor clinked as he drew near.

"Come to finish that witch's work, have you? She doesn't

have the spine to kill me herself?" Her voice sounded as if her teeth were clenched, whether from pain or anger, it was hard to tell. At least until she whirled around to face him.

Her eyes burned with emerald defiance. The moment she recognized him was one of the most beautiful in his life. The anger and challenge morphed instantly into surprise and joy. "Thomas." She struggled to her feet. Had he not hurried over to her, she wouldn't have had enough chain links to reach him.

It was then that he took account of all her injuries. Bruises and slight cuts marred her arms, face, and legs. Her hair was in disarray, and she favored one leg over the other. Delia had not treated him kindly, but she had been beastly to her sister.

How could I have lent one empathetic second to that monster?

Sensing his building fury, or perhaps feeling the tremors it induced in his body, Mia gently redirected his face toward hers and leaned up to kiss him.

It was a kiss tinged in blood, and he had to be so careful, so gentle in returning the pressure. Even so, it was enough to take him, in that brief instant, far from the turmoil and trouble and tumult crashing down all around them.

When they parted, she said, "I heard the commotion ... I was afraid it was time for our executions."

His heart utterly refused to entertain imagining such a thing. "You needn't fear that, so long as I live," he promised.

"What is happening then?" Mia asked.

"The Albarons are attacking the encampment, Baroness," Ilsa called from the entrance to the tent. "Not to be impertinent and interrupt your reunion, my lady, but we must hurry. The battle seems to be drawing to a conclusion, and if either group catches us about, they'll kill us all."

Mia looked up into his eyes and stroked his cheek once more.

Then she stepped away, leaving behind the imagined alcove of the Lowlands inhabited only by them. "We have to get Gregor. Delia has meant him harm from the start, but if we leave him here, she will make his death so torturously painful, these mountains will echo with his cries until the High King returns to reign."

At the last bit, Thomas couldn't help taking extra interest. Though he had pledged himself to the High King's service, Mia had never done so. This was, in fact, the most open declaration of her accepting the High King's role in their world he had heard from her. A far cry from both of them disavowing him entirely at the start of the war.

But he could not linger and pull her back aside to their pocket of peace to discuss it. "Ilsa is right about what will happen if we're seen. Let me retrieve Gregor, and you both work your way to the edge of the camp." Pointing past Ilsa to the dark distance, he added, "If you can, make for the Eigh River. We'll join you there. Depending on the outcome of the battle, we can make for Seabridge in the west or ..." Thomas faltered. There wasn't really an alternative.

If they were where he understood them to be, they were stuck. Caldoness to the east was blocked from access by the high peaks of the Upper Albar Mountain range. Hoarcrest to the northeast would require fording the Eigh River or navigating the Reota Forest. Neither of which was advisable without supplies or warmer clothing. Not to mention, he was working off knowledge of the land from looking at a regional map. Unlike when they fled the Monarchists in Ecthelowall, he was far from versed in the Albaron landscape. He was sure no one else was either.

"Well then, to the Eigh River and Seabridge in the west." Mia reached up and planted a quick kiss on his lips. "Take care, Captain. I have not released you from your duty to me."

"Not for all the Lowlands, my lady." He gave her a mock bow.

Her playful smile at their banter around each's official roles faded, and he saw the real concern beneath it etched into the tensing of her cheeks. But an instant later, she was gone. Slipping with Ilsa off into the night, he hoped, to do just as they had agreed.

He emerged a moment later and surveyed the camp. Ilsa was right. Even hampered by the night, he could tell the Monarchists were being pushed back, their ranks tightening and funneling back into the camp. He had to find Gregor—and fast.

Scanning the camp, Thomas grimaced as he realized he had no idea where they would be keeping his cousin. He regretted sending Ilsa and Mia on. Between their extraordinary powers of observation, surely one of the pair had seen some hint of Gregor's holding place.

A sudden flash of a strange green light arched from the Monarchist's lines and struck deep in the Albaron's advancing columns. A cheer rose up from the Monarchists.

A shiver raced down Thomas's back. That was no natural weapon. He felt it in his bones and in the sudden furious heat of his spiritsword's indignation. Dark magic. Delia must have indeed been well studied in it.

The Albaron line faltered for a moment, looking as if it might break and retreat. But Thomas's eyes were on something else. The flash had illuminated a small makeshift pen for animals belonging to the Monarchist camp. Mainly horses, but also a few mules and, curiously, pigs.

Of course. Where else would be fit for "the little pig"?

Thomas rushed over to the simple split-rail structure and vaulted over the top, landing with a slip into the thick mud already churned up by the assemblage of beasts. Most of the horses were gone, pulled for use in the battle. But there, tied to a post beside a makeshift trough for feeding was a small, crumpled shape. Gregor. His head was down, and he was tightly balled beside the post as a pig snuffled around him.

A cry went up from the distance, wild, and guttural. It came from the Albaron's side and must have been in terror of what powers Delia wielded. Once again, time to act was slipping out of his hands faster than he could lay hold of it.

"Gregor!" Thomas called out, risking both the volume and openness of slogging over in full view.

The boy's head drifted up by fractions, his eyes glassy and unfocused. As Thomas got closer, a terrible stench, distinct from the animals, reached him.

"Gregor?" He asked, bringing his arm up in front of his mouth and nose to ward away the foul odor.

"After they beat me, she made me eat from the trough like the pigs. I wretched it all up until there was nothing left in me."

Amid the cuts and bruises and mud covering Gregor's face, Thomas could make out the evidence of where Gregor had thrown up multiple times. But it was the listlessness in the boy that was more concerning. He had lost more than the contents of his stomach. For someone like Gregor, every shred of his dignity must also now be lost amid the muck and refuse.

Cutting free the ropes with a quick swipe of his burning blade, Thomas hauled the boy to his feet with some difficulty. "Come on, we'll get you cleaned by the river."

The faintest hint of focus returned to his eyes as he resisted walking and was hauled by Thomas toward the pen's exit. "We?" he inquired.

"Mia, Ilsa, and I."

There was a noticeable lifting of his head at the mention of Ilsa. "We have to hurry. Delia wants us all dead!"

Thomas nodded and checked the battle lines. To his shock,

the Albarons had not backed away, but rather, the cry from before must have been to charge. The Monarchist line was shattering as he watched.

"We have to go. Now!"

Gregor seemed to be livening, took one step without Thomas, and collapsed screeching with pain. It was then he noticed Gregor's leg looked awful and misshapen.

"Is it broken?" he asked, horrified by the dirtiness mingling with the blood and torn flesh.

"Yes, but I thought ... somehow ... your armor would heal me. Like Glewdyn's spiritsword did the man in Kirke."

For a few seconds, Thomas gaped at Gregor. He was right. Glewdyn had healed a serious wound inflicted by a Sombra's dagger by using the searing divine heat of his spiritsword. But Thomas did not know if there was some knowledge required for it or simply the sword's power imbued by the High King behind it. "Oh, Gregor," he mumbled.

Gnawing his lip, he watched as the first of the Monarchists reached the camp in flight, running past the pen without noticing them. Thomas hoisted Gregor back up. "What inflicted the wound? Was it something dark that Delia wielded or a common weapon?"

Gregor sniffled.

"Gregor, tell me!" Thomas demanded as two more soldiers dashed past, dozens of feet to their left.

"It was a mule! I tried to be brave. So, I knocked over my guard and ran to mount it to escape. It kicked my leg as I did. I'm a horrid pathetic fool!" Shudders rocked his young body as he sobbed. "Leave me. I'm not worth rescuing."

"What are you on about? Of course you're worth rescuing," Thomas replied tensely, rubbing small circles on the boy's back. He kept a wary eye on the chaos unfolding around them now.

Dozens of monarchists crashed into and over each other to escape. The first of the Albarons were upon them.

Perhaps this is better. A proper rescue by the Albarons.

It was more what he wanted than what he could dare believe, though. Not after Steward Kilkern's betrayal. The truth was, it was pointless now to try. The Albarons were upon them.

He helped Gregor over to the fencing to grip it and held fast to the boy, keeping his shield up in guard. They would not harm Gregor further without first finishing Thomas off.

A trio of soldiers each bearing a long broadsword, claymore by the look of them, halted alongside the pen and took notice of them.

"What da we 'ave 'ere, boys?" one of them, bearded and burly, asked in a thick Albaron brogue. "It looks like these Ecthel piggies are all penned up for tha' slaughter!"

It was then that Thomas noticed another group carrying high an Albaron steward's banner marching into the center of the Monarchist camp and planting it firmly. To Thomas's horror, it belonged to the only steward it couldn't possibly be —Kilkern.

Definitely not a rescue.

"I won't let you harm him, again. If Steward Kilkern wants to hurt him, let him come and face me. Tell him Sir Thomas Fenwrest issues a challenge!"

One of the other soldiers grabbed his fellow blue tartan and silver-suited warrior and shook him. "Leave off! Those are tha' two we were sent to retrieve. The Steward would 'ave a word with them."

Thomas dropped into a defensive stance, ready to make a stand when he caught sight of something that stilled every muscle in him, his very breath caught for an instant.

"Let go of me you brute!" Mia demanded as she was

dragged along by another of the Albarons. Ilsa marched quietly under the guard of three additional Albarons.

"We caught 'em trying to make for the Eigh," the one towing Mia informed the others. He spat. "This one has a surprising amount of fight for a Baroness."

Mia shot Thomas an apologetic look, and he released a shuddering breath. And just like that, their chances of escape were erased, and their hopes for the future dissolved.

12

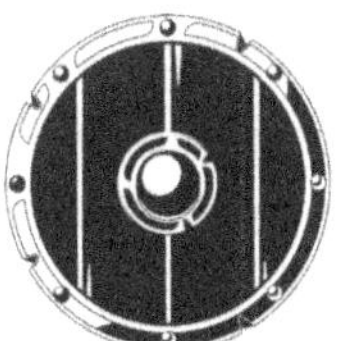

"Perhaps he isn't going to kill us?" Ilsa suggested. Though with much less conviction than when she had put forward the possibility the previous night. At that time, it had seemed plausible. Though the Steward had not seen them personally, the Albarons in his employ were gentler this time. Forceful, but not cruel. They allowed Mia, Gregor, Thomas, and Ilsa to remain in a tent together, and though they confiscated Thomas's spiritsword, they left him his armor and his shield. As hours slipped from deep night into mid-morning, however, the prospects of a warm welcome, of any sort of conviviality, were banished.

"More likely ..." Gregor began and halted, drowsiness and pain strangling his words. "He's trying to ransom us and ... Delia back to Monarch Ilyron."

"That would be a bold move," Mia said with a yawn. Leaning against Thomas, she absently traced the engravings on Thomas's armor with her fingers. She was so close and being intimate with Thomas. Abandoning the decorum of being put together and constant adherence to societal rules was a bad sign. "He would be isolated. Neither allied with Albaron nor the Monarchists. At most he would gain a begrudging payout from a Monarch who might as easily sweep him away once the war is over."

"*Ow!*" Gregor yelped as Ilsa delicately removed the makeshift bandaging they had applied to Gregor's broken leg to replace it with fresh strips torn from her dress.

Ilsa's face was lined with tension highlighted by the pale light sneaking in from the morning of a new day and the glow from Thomas's armor. "Sorry," Ilsa mewled. "It looks infected, you're going to need good medicine and a proper doctor for it to mend."

From beyond the tent flap came a stern voice, "Perhaps then I should have a look at it?"

Into the small space, flanked by two guards bearing torches and two more behind at the flap with halberds was Steward Kilkern. He was garbed in his armor that bore a black swath across part of the otherwise polished cuirass and pauldron. As though something had flash burned and scored it with the residue. His mouth was set in a line, but his features were neither hard nor soft, as though he was merely there and not their betrayer, captor, and potential executioner.

Mia immediately straightened. Putting some space between herself and Thomas. Which earned an eyebrow raise from the Steward. "You needn't insult my intelligence by pretending you're not infatuated with the Captain of your guard. Sir Fenwrest has already confided in me his feelings for you."

Eyes wide and cheeks reddened, Mia shot him a look of reproof. Wincing under her gaze, Thomas replied, "If I'd known what sort of man you are, I wouldn't have told you anything more than what ultimately becomes of traitors and murderers."

One of the guards started to step forward, his hand already raised to backhand Thomas, but Kilkern caught him. "What sort of man am I ... I wonder myself now." He said it almost as though to himself. Focus returned to his gaze after a moment, and he addressed his guard. "Bring the boy. I would have a look at his leg. Clean the others up as best as can be managed and feed them. Then bring them all before me."

He paused as he turned to exit without waiting to see their nods of assent. "Oh, and make sure they see her on their way to my tent."

An hour later they had eaten a simple meal of some cured beef and hard bread. They had been offered some wine, but Thomas refused, wanting to have all his wits about him for what came next. The soldiers tending to them were strangely courteous, if solemn. They did not gloat or seem to take smug satisfaction from the screams of pain Gregor loosed.

Over all of it hung the question of what Kilkern had meant. Who did he want them to see and for what purpose? Did he mean Delia? Was he intending to parade them in defeat before the Queen to further batter their morale before execution?

About an hour after the screams ended, a soldier came into the tent Mia, Thomas, and Ilsa sat in in silence and announced. "The Steward is ready for you. Follow me."

They all filed out, Mia at the front, followed by Ilsa, and Thomas bringing up the back. Overhead, the sun was bright and warm, and the little vale that had seemed so foreboding the other night was vibrant with magenta heather, songs of birds, and a strong seasonal breeze. It was a jarring change. Especially as they walked toward the biggest Albaron tent and suddenly veered toward the middle of camp where a large wooden pole was buried deep in the ground and surrounded by hay. At each side, guards bearing torches looked tensed to ignite the hay.

Tied to the pole was Delia. She'd been placed in a burlap sack such that only her head was exposed. The Albarons had lashed her to the post with thick rope at the shoulders, hips, and ankles. If her face was any indication, the Albarons had been gentle with her, not beating her freely as the Monarchists had them. Even so, her head was cast down, her hair helping to mask whatever glower or grimace she bared for them.

There were no vestiges of the old Delia remaining, so it was difficult for Thomas to work up any sympathy for her plight. At least until his eyes shifted to focus on Mia, and though her expression was as solid as granite, he knew beneath it all her heart must be adrift in a sea of sorrow and pain. He had lost his entire family in a single night. She was losing the last member of hers over and over in ever more heartbreaking and horrific ways.

A few moments later, they were at the big tent, Mia's eyes still on the pyre built around her sister. With abrupt finality, she broke her gaze and entered the tent at the soldiers' bidding. Inside was a throne, lightweight, portable. A table of similar transportable nature bore a large map of the region depicting primarily topographical features, though there were a smattering of cities on it. A cursory glance allowed Thomas to note at least four of the seven castle cities that dominated the corresponding stewardships of Albaron.

A few feet to the table's left was Gregor, held up by two guards, a thick white cloth wrapped around his injured leg. It was clear he was in pain, but he did not look any worse for wear than when they had been parted. His cheeks had more color, in fact, which Thomas took to be a good sign. Both for the boy and their prospects of surviving the day.

Looking intently at the map, Steward Kilkern's attention

did not shift to them as they entered, though he did speak to them. "I trust my men cared for you with dignity and compassion?"

No one answered at first, not until the Steward looked up, an eyebrow arched. Mia spoke for them, "They did."

He nodded. "Far better treatment than the Queen has received. I take it you saw well what state she is in?"

"She is nobody's queen," Mia asserted in a flush of anger. Quickly she regained her composure and, through tight lips, said, "But yes. I saw her. Do you intend to burn us if we do not pay a ransom as well? The Restoration will surrender no such fee, I assure you."

Kilkern's eyes narrowed. "I have no desire for any 'fee,' ransom or otherwise. Your sister is dangerous. Truly a witch, if you did not already know."

Mia seemed to mull over this information, shooting Thomas a quick look to which he gave a faint nod. How versed in the dark powers of such creatures she was, he could not know. From the spell she attempted on him and Ilsa, and his memory of the paralyzing poisons used on him and Gregor in Ecthelowall, there was little doubt she had crossed into the arcane and evil.

"And you are a traitor," Mia blurted out, stunning Thomas and eliciting a gasp from a nearby guard, who raised his halberd's pointed spear tip toward her.

The steward motioned for the man to lower his weapon. "You are right, I suppose." Taking in a deep breath, Kilkern gestured to the table, "Take a look at this map—what do you see?"

Mia looked at him as if the Steward was insane, and Thomas had to wonder if that were the case as well. She then peered at the map and commented, "It's the geography of the region. With a few cities and troop positions marked."

"Aye. Those aren't just any troop positions. They're the armies personally attached to both Viceroy Ecthelion and Monarch Ilyron. Do you notice anything about them?"

Now Thomas's eyes were fixed on the map. How had he overlooked it the first time he observed the map? There was a marker right beside Dirkforge in the south. The Viceroy was supposed to be safe there, hidden away with an army of only the most loyal in the Restoration Army's ranks and overseeing the forging and distribution of weapons to the key positions and armies of the war. How did Steward Kilkern know this?

"How do you know that?" Mia demanded, voicing what Thomas had only been bold enough to think.

"Not that I owe you an explanation, but as a physician, you never act in ignorance, when possible. I have spies in Ilyron's inner circle, and certainly my men have no issues with surveilling the lands of their birth. It is because I know their positions that we are standing here. So, tell me, what do you see? What is of significance?"

"I do not have the patience nor the will to play games," Mia seethed. "So, get to whatever sick torments you have for me, or send my handmaiden back to retrieve whatever it is you want from us."

Kilkern rubbed his face and started to speak but was interrupted by Gregor. "Ilyron is too far north," he commented. His voice was hoarse from his cries of pain earlier. "It does not make sense for him to be moving on Hoarcrest. It's a terrible icy mess, even during spring, and the mountains will bar him from advancing on Caldoness."

Thomas once more was astonished at his blindness. "Worse than that, the Albarons know those mountains. The Laird's archers would be on the heights of every pass, picking his army to the bone like carrion fowl."

"Mm. Carrion, yes. That is something to discuss," Kilkern

acknowledged cryptically. "Well observed, both of you, for two so young. Yes, the Monarch's movements are peculiar. As are his Queen's."

"She was coming to secure your tribute," Mia accused. "The blood price for throwing in with the Monarch."

"That is what I allowed her to believe, yes. But the Queen is well aware of where the Viceroy is right now."

Thomas shot a look at Ilsa, whose eyes were cast down, her expression best described as brooding. Clearing his throat, Thomas countered, "Then why was she questioning Ilsa and me about his whereabouts?"

Kilkern nodded as if it were a small detail. "That is an odd play, yes. Were she not a witch, I would think more of it. Her games are of the most twisted sort now. Perhaps it was simply to break your spirit. Cause you to betray what you can least afford to and thereby destroy you more fully than simply breaking your body ever could.

"I'm certain, however, that she knows where the Viceroy is," he drew out the last words as he stalked forward and put down another marker of the same color as Ilyron's. It was settled at Daggerpointe. "Because her kinsman landed their entire army here and are marching on Dirkforge and the Fisure Fens as we speak."

"That's impossible!" Mia protested. "With the pressure from Libertias, she can't afford to redirect a significant force from Emeral."

Whether Kilkern had truly known the Viceroy's whereabouts until that moment, Thomas couldn't say. The older man's face was stony and there seemed almost a tinge of pity in the crinkling around his eyes. "Child, I assure you it isn't just possible, it is the reality we face. The armies of Libertias are indispensable to us, but they aren't turning the tide of the war—merely locking it into a stalemate."

"But surely our numbers," Gregor insisted. "No one has said a word of things not being in our favor."

Now Kilkern did look unambiguously empathetic. "Only the highest nobles have been informed of the full extent of the war's stalling. There are couriers bringing strange accounts of the Monarchist forces fighting past the point of wounds that would down any normal man, as though they are blind to their injuries. Ferocious, unflinching, such as even the Ord and Dag Votere berserkers of old had never dreamed to be."

"Carrion," Thomas concluded, dreading the word even as he said it. Often at night his dreams would be haunted by his memories of such soldiers who acted as if they were past pain, caught in state between life and death, their will utterly stripped from them.

The Steward nodded. "Yes. You told me of them, and till last night, I did not believe they could exist. I do now. And I fear our numbers are not sufficient to overcome such creatures."

Ilsa cleared her throat, heretofore silent. "What has changed your mind, Your Honor?"

Sucking in a sharp breath, Kilkern rocked back and gripped the table. His jaw tensed and his eyes fixed on the table. He didn't answer.

After several seconds, Mia chided. "Of course, no answer. You weave fine tales and play a dangerous game of walking both sides of this war, Steward. You're foolish if you think after all we lost, we would just—"

Slamming his fist on the table, the usually stoic Kilkern snarled back, "Do not speak to me of loss. I allowed you all to be taken and played the part of a traitor to lure the Queen into a trap and discover the real aims of the Monarchists' movements in Albaron.

"If I'm guilty of a folly, it is that I had intended to keep you and the boy-heir in my protection as wards and only allow

Thomas and your handmaiden to be taken. Of course, no such thing was tenable, and yes, I did risk all of your lives to arrive at the truth. But if you will stop hoarding it like Tislatnean primuses did treasure, we could move forward."

In the silence after Kilkern's outburst, Thomas felt a pressure. Firm and insistent, build in his chest. Closing his eyes he pleaded that the High King work it all out, because he knew Mia would not be in favor of what he was about to do. "Delia mentioned Wyvares when she first arrived at Kilkern's Redoubt. If that was really where she was taking us, could that be part of their plan?."

"Wyvares?" Kilkern's face went slack, some of the color draining from it. After several seconds, he seemed to compose himself and drifted toward Thomas. "She told you her plans outright?"

"No more than she told you. She spent most of our time trying to trick us into revealing the Viceroy's location by tempting us with things she thought we'd want."

"And you're certain she wasn't beguiling you? Her plans genuinely include Wyvares?"

"Yes." Thomas shot a look at Ilsa for confirmation. But the handmaiden was looking at the ground, her lips pressed in a tight line. Was she feeling bitterness over their trial, because she had almost given in? If so, he would have to comfort her later. It had been hard for him to refuse Delia's offers, even absent the spell.

Thomas's attention was jerked back to the Steward forcefully by Kilkern clearing his throat. With all the severity of the grave, the old physician looked out on each of them in turn and said, "Then, my dear children, we are all doomed."

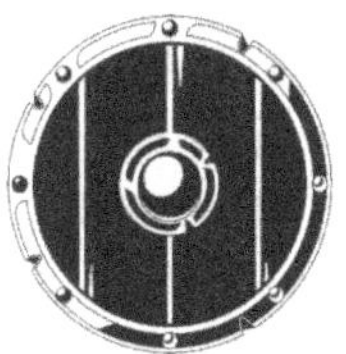

"Doomed?" Gregor mewled.

Mia crossed her arms over her chest, past the point of decorum, and openly vented her temper. "What do you mean? And don't give us any more of your esoteric nonsense about your intentions and schemes happening around us."

If Mia was past any sense of diplomacy, Kilkern's expression betrayed that he may have been past the point of hope. His eyes were distant, and the despondence weighing him down came out in every word he spoke. "I'm afraid if you want me to produce physical evidence of what I'm about to relate, I cannot. Nor can I promise to offer only sage words well passed by many mouths over generations. We in Albaron have feared Wyvares since the nation's founding.

"The Lowlands used to be wilder and darker than they are presently—at least, so the old tales tell us. In them, it is the servants of the High King bearing his light that chased out the monstrous and wicked things, forcing them into the shadows. Among them are creatures, such as the wyvern."

"Stop," Mia demanded. "Are you seriously about to tell me

the reason you allowed us to be taken with every possibility of execution and are holding us prisoner now, is because you're scared of imaginary beasts?"

"Not imaginary," Thomas demurred. "Anargen told me his mentor Sir Cinaed sacrificed himself fighting a wyvern in Stormridge."

The look Mia shot him was mixed. There was certainly annoyance from him, interrupting and seemingly siding with Kilkern, as well his challenge that, once again, what she believed about the Lowlands was incomplete. There was also a degree of thoughtfulness there because of all that had passed between them, what they were to each other. That alone spared him a sharp rebuke.

"I also thought them fables until two nights ago" Kilkern seemed to perceive the conflict in Mia. But he deflated before he could elaborate further, a twinge of something bitter rendering him listless.

"What happened two nights ago?" Mia pressed.

Kilkern looked down at his map, braced his hand on the table, only to suddenly clench his hand in a fist as if being buffeted by unseen waves. "I saw sorcery for the first time, with my eyes," he admitted, his voice hitching at the end.

"What sort of *sorcery*?" Thomas prompted, albeit gently.

"That witch outside—" Tears entered his eyes only to be shut off from falling by the rage twisting his features. "—used her dark arts to kill my son."

Reflexively, Thomas looked back toward the tent flap, to where Delia was bound to the stake, ready to be burned at a moment's notice. This shouldn't have mattered to his opinion of her. After all, she had killed her father, would have killed her loving sister without blinking. Yet it did, somehow. As if it put her still further out of the reach of the light, ever the deeper within the shadows. Kilkern had no other heirs. The suffering was both personal to Kilkern and, more broadly, his subjects. Losing his son meant his people would likely face upheaval and a struggle over who would rise to replace the Steward at his death.

"You ... have my condolences," Mia offered after several seconds of silence. What could they possibly say in the face of such a loss?

"You may keep them if you will, instead, give me your attention and a modicum of trust."

"Trust is costly," she replied. "But, yes. I can, *we* can, give you that much."

Breathing out a sigh of resignation, Kilkern continued. "Early in the settling of Albaron, our ancestors faced down a brood of wyvern in the Upper Albar Mountains along with covens of witches that seemed to caretake and reverence them in one. Over decades, the Knights of Light overcame all but one wyvern, which resided in a region north and east of here. A secluded upthrust in the mountains there makes a small ring valley, and many of our stories end there with the creature taking up residence and nothing more. Some of the oldest, most fanciful tales include the beast being sealed. Some say by elves come to aid the Knights. Some say it was by the last coven of witches, plotting to use the beast to exact revenge for the Knights banishing them from the lands they once held sway over.

"I discounted it all as fairy tales and nonsense, until I saw the Queen of Ecthelowall summon and use dark sorcery to destroy my child. If the witches I had equally dismissed as rot are flesh and blood, then I fear the wyvern to be real as well. Whether sealed or unsealed, if a witch and whatever dark force the Monarch himself represents were to gain as a weapon the fire and fangs of a wyvern—with our forces already so tenuously holding our lines—the Devastation plague, the carrion soldiers, and then terrifying beasts straight from our blackest nightmares we've long tried to forget ..."

Kilkern wandered back to his seat and dropped into it heavily. He shook his head. "It would be the end, of all of us."

Thomas swallowed with some difficulty. For him, there was no doubt that the stories were true. Kilkern had not stared down a werebeast, been accosted by its foul odor, watched its wicked eyes gleam with bloodlust. Nor seen a goblin and its unspeakable evil, an oppressive darkness that was felt as much as observed. Until one encounters the dark things of the world firsthand, it is perilously easy to pretend them myths and fancy.

He realized Mia was looking at him, her eyes searching. She had seen those dark beings as well. Been hunted by each, marked for suffering and slaughter by them. In her emerald gaze he could see her pleading for some sign that she could dismiss this account. That in this one instance, perhaps the stories were all just that—stories. That some monsters really did remain in the minds of storytellers and frightened children. Once more, Thomas swallowed with some difficulty and closed his eyes.

No. His heart felt the warm, firm pressure that he'd come to trust with his life. Even his armor felt hotter, just at the mention of such things. Not all old tales were true, but this one, like far too many dismissed long ago, was, and that meant when he opened his eyes, he had to give the woman he loved a nod. Slow and heartbreaking, because he saw the immediate flush of dread it induced. Quickly masked, but undeniable.

Mia reoriented her attention from Thomas, and they both watched the steward, who was still sitting sullen on his throne. Perhaps weighing how long he would yet live to sit upon it. Months? Weeks?

"Your Honor," Mia began, her words tight, clipped. "Were we to ... believe your stories, what do we do next?"

For an instant, there was a strident chord of panic racing through the old man's face before he reined it in. Schooling his features, much as Mia had done—a skill essential to their stations and upbringing. With the candor of a physician, Kilkern said, "There is precious little that can be. My sources say the army Ilyron brings is too much for my retainers to handle alone. The nearest army that could be of aid is in Caldoness, but it will be needed to reinforce Dirkforge."

"Then, we've already lost?" Gregor stated as much as asked.

Kilkern shot up from his seat. "No, not yet. We know the Queen was headed for Wyvares as well, rather than oversee here people's campaign against Viceroy Ecthelion. If she would leave such an important assault for this errand, then perhaps she is indispensable to it. Witches were often involved in beguiling the beasts in old tales. What if the Monarch needs her for some ritual to gain the creature's loyalty?"

"That is a bit of a leap," Mia replied, softly. "My sister wasn't born a witch."

Nodding, but already clearly working through things internally, Kilkern continued, "If we pull her south, then the Monarch may not be able to move forward with his plan. The Upper Albar Mountains would be a barrier to him, tie up his large force. That could buy us time to defeat the Emeralan Army coming against Dirkforge and regroup. In fact, it may be the very sort of victory we need to put the Monarch back onto the defensive."

"That's awfully ambitious, Your Honor," Gregor critiqued. He started to add something else but winced from a jolt of pain.

Thomas thought he could guess what Gregor would have said and spoke up. "It would also mean an angry Ilyron with a large force would be free to strike out against Hoarcrest and Seabridge without much hope for either getting aid. Though

Seabridge might hold out, Hoarcrest and its Stewardship could be lost entirely."

Mulling it for a moment, Kilkern rejoined, "It is the physician's arts which teach you must apply the tourniquet, even if it means the patient loses a limb. Better that than lose their life."

It was so cold, so twisted in its rationality when applied to the hundreds and thousands living in those regions, it brought Thomas up short. Seabridge was even a part of Kilkern's Stewardship, the lands he was sworn to defend above all others. How could he have ever been this man's friend? Certainly, the Steward had put on some degree of a façade, but Thomas should've seen through it, seen the chink in the deceit's armor. Was that not part of being a Knight of Light? Worse, did he have a similar blindness toward others' true natures?

His gaze drifted to Mia, and he could see she was deliberating. When she caught his attention on her, her brows knit for a moment before she flipped her curling red tresses and huffed to Kilkern. "Then there is no other choice."

"Mia?" he pleaded.

She held up a hand, without looking at him. "Steward, if you are truly our ally all along, we need you to take us to Dirkforge and warn the Viceroy. Immediately."

Kilkern gave a curt nod and said, "We break camp and make for the Fisure Fens before dusk."

Thomas's core felt hollowed out. Had Mia really dismissed the people of the north—dismissed him—so easily? If that was the only right course forward, why did he feel a deep, lingering misgiving about it all?

14

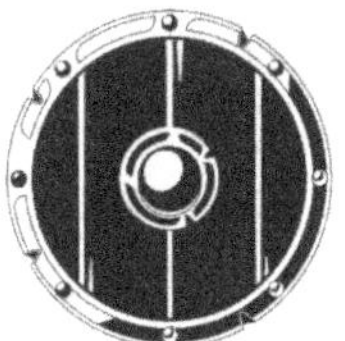

Dirkforge was both more and less than Thomas expected. The heath of the northern lands felt far removed from the wetlands surrounding him now. From atop the battlements, he had a solid view of the lush, verdant grasses and shrubs, shaking in the breeze far into the distance. Dotting the Fisure Fens were little hovels where bog iron was extracted and a few farms had been started at the periphery of the wetlands. His father's lands had been the Isle of Fens, which, while similar, had become overexploited. The land over cultivated and eroded. The failure of the peat exports and crops that had made the Isle of Fens at one time an incredibly rich and important march within Ecthelowall was one of the driving factors that had ruined Thomas's father and ultimately led to his parent's deaths.

Thomas turned back from looking outward toward the interior of Dirkforge. Developed over the years, the battlements now sat inside the fens rather than at their edge. The interior town and castle proper were located on a sort of island at its center with a rather angular architecture to everything from the barbicans to the keep. Impressive for its age and place in Albaron culture as its chief source of smelted iron and smithed goods, Thomas couldn't fight the pang of grief that came with seeing its stones still standing, still thriving. Why had his home languished and disintegrated while this place continued to grow and excel as it had for centuries?

His gaze swept directly downward. Restoration soldiers were beginning to gather on the catwalks and platforms built over the wetlands between the outermost wall he was on and the island. Even with the added soldiers Kilkern's Redoubt and those Caldoness were willing to spare, this would be a close battle. Somewhere, just beyond the fens Thomas had looked out on, were Emeralan soldiers preparing to attack. Perhaps it was wrong to envy Dirkforge's success. In a few days' time, it could all be an utterly ruined waste and everyone inside dead.

"You don't hold much hope for our success?" a quiet voice broke into Thomas's ponderings.

Starting, he staggered back into a parapet. "Ilsa? What are you doing up here?" He glanced down the wall and didn't spot any of the soldiers who should be between himself and the nearest tower. She must have snuck up in between their changing out or they were pulled back to help with the lower defenses.

"I know it's not proper for a handmaiden such as myself to be up here," she answered softly but with an edge of ire. "However, the Baroness sent me to summon you."

"Oh." He leaned heavily against the parapet. "Thank you."

Ilsa's hands were folded in front of her, and she looked on him expectantly.

"You can go on ahead," he said. "I know my way. I just need ..." he sighed. What did he need? It had been days since he'd spent any more time with Mia than absolutely necessary. Their differing opinions on sacrificing the northern stewardships had created a rift. One he had not attempted to close—wasn't certain he should close.

"Hmm." Ilsa's eyes narrowed for an instant. She dropped down to sit on the stone between the parapets. "You're avoiding her."

It wasn't a question, nor was it barbed as an accusation. "I suppose so." Thomas crossed his arms over his chest.

From his peripheral vision, he could see Ilsa nodding. "I understand. You're preparing yourself for what comes next. One way or another, this battle is going to impact the direction of the war. Either ending all of us or putting us on the path to victory. One where commoners like us will always be kept in our place, far from beside those we serve. No matter how much we care for them."

Thomas arched his brow at her. That was scary perceptive. For an instant, he was worried he had been so easy to read that Mia might have noticed.

Ilsa smiled up at him, wistful. "I have the same dilemma with Gregor. He cares about me, but nothing can ever come of it." She huffed. "I'm just a handmaiden, and if the Restoration succeeds, he may be Monarch someday. Loving him in return would only make life harder for both of us. It's easier to keep my distance than to reach for what we can never have together."

"I'm sorry, I've been so preoccupied, I hadn't realized you both ..." He trailed off. Nothing he could say right now would change either of their situations. If he was honest with himself, Ilsa had already put to words for him what he was doing out here. What he'd been doing for days, diminishing the sharp pain of parting by letting his bond with Mia slowly wither instead of being suddenly cut off.

Standing, Ilsa reached out a hand brushed it along Thomas's cheek, startling him again. She smiled. "Sorry. I thought there might have been a tear coming, but it looks like you've already decided this, haven't you?"

He was about to answer when he caught sight of Gregor standing about halfway between them and the tower. The boy was on a crutch, his injured leg swollen, an infection barely kept in check by the best of Steward Kilkern's arts. Even from this distance, Thomas could tell his cousin was upset. "Gregor?" he called out.

The boy turned and hobbled toward the tower he'd come from without answering.

It took half a second to realize what he must have seen, or rather what Gregor must have thought he'd seen—Ilsa meeting Thomas atop the battlements in secret and her caressing his cheek after he'd been avoiding Mia.

"No, no. Gregor, wait!"

Ilsa stood to block him. "You know, it would be better for us both if you let him go and stay here with me instead. Instead of prolonging our suffering, maybe we can help each other move forward."

Thomas shook his head. What Ilsa said made sense, but deep within, as much as he was binding and blocking his heart's aches, he could not help it. He had to set this right. "Some things are worth enduring the pain." He dashed down the stone wall, pausing just before entering the tower to look back at Ilsa. She was walking along the wall toward a gatehouse in the courtyard.

Strangely, he half expected her to be watching him. Her voice had almost been pleading a moment ago. Shaking his head to clear it, Thomas entered the tower and wound his way along its steps, catching Gregor just as the boy was making a corner within the tower to start down the next round of stairs.

"Gregor, stop!"

"*No!*" Gregor growled, the edge of a sob marring his words. "Keep away from me!"

Ignoring the demand, Thomas edged around his cousin, dodging a swipe from the crutch Gregor aimed at him. Thomas managed to get in front of him and bolster the younger boy, who must have forgotten he needed that crutch for his balance.

Gregor realized a half second later Thomas was holding him up, because he pulled his other hand off the wall of the stairwell and gave Thomas a left hook. Fortunately, Gregor wasn't in full fighting shape and didn't have the leverage to deliver much of a punch. Even so, it was an emotional shock that hit much harder.

"What in the Lowlands was that for?" Thomas demanded.

Red-cheeked with tears starting to come, Gregor snapped, "It's not enough you had Mia wrapped around your finger. You to steal Ilsa's heart too? I can't believe she was right about you!"

Gregor stumbled a bit, trying to push past Thomas, or push him down the stairs, Thomas wasn't clear on which. "Hey, hey. Simmer down. I'm not trying to 'steal Ilsa's heart.'" He wanted to say if anyone was wound it was him to Mia's fingers, but that kind of admission would make extricating himself from them that much harder.

"Right, just like you don't wish you were a noble again, so you could swoop in and steal my inheritance and crown?"

The accusation was as ugly as the expression Gregor wore saying it and Thomas was sorely tempted to let the boy drop. If it wouldn't possibly lead to him breaking other bones, Thomas might have allowed it. "Steal your inheritance and crown? Are you insane?"

Another failed swipe from Gregor was his answer.

"I'm not trying usurp you," Thomas insisted. "I was just up here clearing my thoughts, and Ilsa came to let me know the Baroness sent for me. That's all. There's nothing between Ilsa and me. I have absolutely no interest in trying to take what's yours.

"I mean, come on, Gregor. How many times have I saved your life? Including right now?"

The last bit drew Gregor up short and looked at how steep the stairs were and how very much he was leaning on Thomas. "I ... just ... I ..."

Thomas sighed. "Just tell me what you risked your life coming up here to tell me, and hang on. I'll carry you back down."

Hoisting him up in the crooks of his arms, Thomas began down the stairs before Gregor could protest. It concerned him how light the boy felt. He had grown some inches in the past few months but lost a lot of weight. His latest illness wasn't helping.

Somewhere around the halfway point, Gregor muttered, "Sorry. The Viceroy asked me to call for you. He wants to speak with you in his quarters."

"Oh? Did His Honor say what he needs?"

"No," Gregor replied slowly, in such a way that made Thomas suspicious that the other wasn't being truthful.

"Okay. Mind if I bring you along?"

"It depends ... what was Ilsa doing on the battlements with you?"

Oh. Right.

Reaching the bottom of the tower and sucking in a deep breath as he adjusted Gregor's weight in his arms, Thomas answered, "I already told you. She was informing me the Baroness also summoned me."

Gregor frowned. "Brr, did you pack some Hoarcrest ice and bring it south with you?"

At that Thomas had to laugh. It wasn't a wholesome healthy

one. More like one that took the place of other emotions and reactions that would have torn him apart too much to free from the confines he'd stowed them in. "I suppose I did." He stopped for just a second and looked at his cousin. "I don't begrudge you for inheriting what my father squandered. But we both know without a title, it doesn't matter how much I love her. When everything is decided in this war, I'll either see her die or have to watch from the guardhouse as she's betrothed to someone else who does bear a title. And I can't bear the thought of either."

It was hard to read the conflict in Gregor's face, and since he didn't say anything, Thomas got back to walking. After a few pauses to rest ,they were back inside the castle courtyard, which had a special passage out to the outermost battlements. It struck Thomas how foolhardy Gregor had been in his current state to try to make the trek from the Viceroy's quarters all the way to the battlement.

"The Viceroy didn't send you to speak to me, did he?" Thomas inquired, continuing to walk, not looking at Gregor directly.

Grimacing, Gregor took a long pause before answering, "I came to get you of my own accord ... I ..."

"Does the Viceroy really need me then?" Thomas asked, trying not to get annoyed either way.

"Yes, he does. I'm sure someone else was dispatched. They just don't know you like I do."

Given what Gregor had accused Thomas of minutes ago, Thomas did well to just grumble a "Humph."

Gregor tensed in Thomas's arms and tugged until he got his cousin to look at him. "Listen, Thomas. About before. I'm sorry, but can I ask something of you?"

"You mean besides devoting a fair portion of my next few hours to making sure you haven't really done yourself injury through over-exertion? Before I must rush to my station for the battle ahead?"

The boy winced, and Thomas took a breath, pushing aside his anger and bitterness. "I'm sorry as well. Of course, Gregor. What can I do for you?"

"Take us to the Viceroy, before you go to see Mia."

Shrugging, Thomas replied, "At your request, Heir Apparent."

15

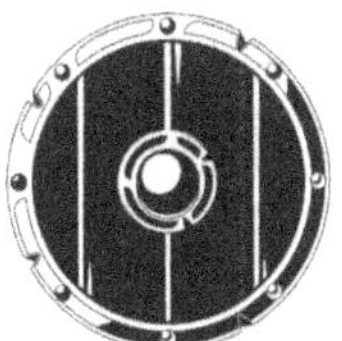

Thomas waited in a sitting room, anxiety wringing him. Gregor had opted to not protest the order from the guards at Ecthelion's chamber doors for him to wait outside. It seemed a strange request, given he must have been within earshot of Ecthelion earlier that day. More rankling, though, was Gregor's insistence that Thomas wait until after speaking with the Viceroy to go to Mia.

Keeping her in wait would mean an apology, which would beg others that Thomas did not want to give, because any forgiveness she granted him would only be a step in the wrong direction for them. He was certain he would love her until the day he died, but the moment this conflict ended, all he would have left is his love and society would demand more of any real suitor for her.

Never mind whatever it was the Viceroy had to say that would complicate things. Perhaps Thomas was being reprimanded for failing to keep her and Gregor safe at Kilkern's Redoubt or he was being reassigned to some other location in the war, away from Mia. The distance the latter provided might help with letting go of her, but only after the war was concluded. Until then, every moment of not being able to be there for her, to safeguard her life with his own, would-be torture.

In that way, this waiting was a microcosm of it. How long had he been sitting here, waiting for the Ecthelion to come out of the Viceroy's study and receive him? Ten minutes? Fifteen? A half hour? There was only so much more time Thomas could spare and then he would have to leave if he wanted to see Mia at all before the battle, which would decide the fate of the war, began.

Thomas stood, laced his fingers behind his head, and paced. Surely the Viceroy wouldn't keep him in suspense just to deliver devastating news like he was being dismissed from service and would have to wait with the citizens of Dirkforge while the battle raged. Helpless and wracked with worry.

A guard gave him a wary glance that indicated he didn't like the teen's nervous energy. Thomas sat again, lacing his fingers again to keep from fidgeting. After a minute, he laid his forehead on his forearm, struggling to keep himself together.

A nip of heat forced him to pull back. He saw some inscriptions glowing brighter than usual on the rebrace he wore, the source of the heat.

Seek first the High King's kingdom and his just oaths, and all else you need will be provided.

Thomas leaned back into the chair slowly. In the midst of all that had happened, he hadn't kept up with his training as a Knight of Light. He had been slowly sacrificing that time to one task or another ever since they helped rescue Viceroy Ecthelion and the Viscount of Libertias from the werebeasts and Sombra assassin over a year ago. Spare time had become non-existent since their capture at Kilkern's Redoubt.

He drew in a few calming breaths, feeling the warmth of the divine armor's flames course through him. His mind had been on literally anything and everything but his oaths to the High King. What and where his lord would have him to be focused. Thomas had not seen him since that initial vision, but he knew how to determine his will. Like on the battlements earlier, when he'd followed the directing rather than his own impulses. It didn't mitigate his negligence, but at least he hadn't drifted so far away that he could not see the path back.

Viceroy Ecthelion emerged from his study minutes later. Long enough for Thomas to place things in perspective and reimagine the invisible structure and strictures he had placed around his heart. He stood and bowed to the Viceroy.

The tall spindly man with hair rapidly graying stepped forward, waving his guards to leave them. He straightened his dark green waistcoat and clapped. "Sir Fenwrest, a hale evening, ever before the dawn of Ecthelowall's Commonwealth." A gentle smile played on his lips.

Thomas tried to keep from betraying his confusion, "Hale evening, ever before the dawn of Ecthelowall's Commonwealth," he repeated. "Your Honor is confident this is a precipitous day for our people's good." He left off his reservations at such a free and confident declaration. Thomas had found peace, but not prescience as to the outcome of the looming battle.

"Your candor is refreshing." The Viceroy patted Thomas on the back and gestured for him to sit at the large oak table that filled much of the waiting room. The Viceroy then seated himself. "I'm told my messenger was not successful in locating you, but your cousin was—he has not injured himself further, has he?"

"It's too soon to know for certain," Thomas admitted. "I plan to bring him to Steward Kilkern to examine him. With your approval, that is, Your Honor." The earlier possibility of Thomas's complete dismissal seemed unlikely now, but not impossible.

"Actually, I have already ordered some of my guards to see to that very task. I'm aware our time is short, so I will get straight to the point." Ecthelion steepled his fingers, his lips pursed as if building up the verve for what he was about to say. He splayed his hands outward. "I have never thanked you for your part in rescuing me from the Sombra and helping to forge the vital alliance we now have with Libertias.

"Nor have I commended you for the courage, patience, and perseverance you showed safeguarding Baroness Sornfold and your cousin. I understand you were forced to survive many weeks in the wild, pinned down by forces you could not overcome alone, and you did so with a fortitude that inspired both your charges."

Thomas shook his head. "You don't have to thank me, Your Honor. It was all by the High King's favor."

"Oh, indeed. That you are a loyal Knight of Light is without doubt integral to what transpired, but do not discount that it was you the High King placed there for such a time. And all of this is to say nothing of the courage and skill you displayed in getting us off Emeral during Delia Sornfold's first betrayal.

"But I'm already saying far more than needs to be. I have a very simple proposition for you, and one I have not arrived at lightly."

Please don't send me away. Please don't send me away.

Ecthelion must have picked up on tension in Thomas's face, because he drummed his fingers on the table. "You need not fear. I believe what I'm offering is a good thing. At least, I hope you will take it as such. In addition to being aware of all your noble deeds, I'm also well acquainted with your father's ignoble ones. Deeds which cost him his life and you the Barony of Isle of Fens. Because of it, you have lost much and stand to lose more if there be light in days to come."

The Viceroy fixed Thomas with such a pointed stare that Thomas knew he was referring to losing Mia if they won the war. "The High King is good. In giving and taking away, I serve his pleasure in each," Thomas replied, his throat tight. It was not an easy proclamation to make, and holding true to it was no simple matter. All the same, he knew enough as a Knight that it was true and he must embrace it.

Ecthelion pointed at him and said, "See, there. That is what I'm speaking of. That is the nobility I need in ... my heir."

Thomas leaned away, confusion growing the longer Ecthelion stared at him fixedly without further explanation. "You want me to help redeem Monarch Ilyron? To teach him virtue?"

"No, no," Ecthelion shook his head emphatically and pinched the bridge of his nose. "Normally, I have more finesse in my speech. Blunt as a cudgel, what I want is for you to take his place ... I want to adopt you as my son, and on my death, confer to you the title Baron of Halifax."

Whatever schooling Thomas had ever been able to apply to his features failed him utterly. His mouth dropped open. "Your Honor?"

A wry smile quirked up one side of Ecthelion's mouth. "You deserve the honors that were stripped of you, and frankly, I will not live forever. If there is to be any hope of Ecthelowall surviving after this war, the nobility cannot have further cause to fight one another. Squabbling over one of the most preeminent marches is a good way to ensure wounds we incur never heal."

Leaning forward and gripping Thomas's forearm, Ecthelion took on a more tender tone. "Whether you know it or not, Thomas Fenwrest, you have a healer's heart. Gregor and Mia are evidence of that. You brought out the best in each of them. I believe you could do the same for Ecthelowall as a whole, if given the chance."

Thomas looked down at Ecthelion's hand, still too shocked to process what he was hearing. "I ... but ... Gregor. I could never be noble again. I would be a rival for Gregor."

Ecthelion shook his head. "No. Gregor will always have the closer claim to the Monarch's throne, which I do understand will be restored, no matter who wins the war. Whatever my hopes for it, the Commonwealth is at an end. Ecthelowall needs a Monarch for now, and one day, that will be Gregor Fenwrest. You, however, will be restyled as Thomas Halifax. My family's crest and lineage will become yours. Much will be required of you, and your responsibility to all as Baron of Halifax will be enormous. But you will not be asked to bear that crown. Remember, I'm seeking not only your reward but peace for all Ecthelowall. My motives are not purely benevolent, and the ends have all been fully considered."

Still gaping, Thomas watched as the Viceroy stood, retrieved a rolled parchment, some wax, and a seal. Returning to the table, he unrolled the document. Swooping dark calligraphy spelled out words Thomas was beyond the hope of comprehending at the moment. Ecthelion seemed to sense this and explained, "This is the official writ ordering the registries of the nobility in Ecthalon to be updated. If you sign it with me, you will be my son in the eyes of Ecthelowall for all posterity." Swallowing with some difficulty, emotion suddenly shattered Ecthelion's disciplined control over his expressions. "You lost a father. I lost a son. Through this, we both may have a fresh chance at a future with each."

Is this really happening? I must be dreaming.

But no, he was here, sitting at a table with the leader of his people, being offered exactly what he wanted most. This sort of thing usually required fairies with wands or magical animals who grant wishes. Things that truly were the stuff of imagination, so far removed from the hard realities that had battered them down over and over. Wasn't there an army amassed just beyond their defenses? A war being fought both here and farther than Thomas had ever dared travel? Perhaps that in itself was evidence enough this was real. No dream would dare overlay such divergent threads.

If this was real, then why wasn't his mouth moving, shouting, "Yes!" for him? Or his head nodding? Why was he frozen?

Ecthelion's countenance fell some, not quite to disappointment, but certainly a deep concern. "You aren't interested in my offer?"

An anxious swell that it could be rescinded gripped Thomas, and he blurted out, "No, no, Your Honor. It's not that ... I just ..."

What was he thinking? Was the High King forbidding it? Thomas didn't think so. This wasn't the inward pressure from without that he was accustomed to when the much bigger and greater High King spoke his will into the deepest parts of Thomas's heart and mind. Whatever held him back was of his contriving.

"You have lived as a commoner for many years," Ecthelion observed. "It would be understandable if the responsibilities and expectations of rejoining the nobility would be unnerving."

Thomas shook his head. "It's not that, Your Honor. I was prepared for that by my parents. Perhaps the only thing my father did prepare me for."

Leaning back in his seat and bringing his hand to his mouth

thoughtfully, Ecthelion mused. "You do not wish to abandon your family name?"

That was perhaps the last of his concerns in the Lowlands. The name Fenwrest would seem to some a blessing, but to him it was just as easily used in curses. His father hadn't been a good man, and the only thing of worth beyond teaching Thomas to bury his emotions and carry himself with inflated sense of dignity was the Fenwrest name. Along with its grief and its shame. Everything of value, everything that had helped to shape Thomas was from Hurstwell's rearing and the High King's transforming.

A strangled groan came out of Thomas's mouth. "I ... I suppose, a part of me is just sorry that I wasn't reclaimed from my broken family name by Sir Hurstwell, Your Honor. All I learned of chivalry and honor—lessons I'm sure he taught me that are still soaking into me with time—all of that was Hurstwell."

"I see." Ecthelion's brows knitted and he looked thoughtful for a time. "What would Hurstwell tell you now?"

"To stop being sentimental, thick-headed, and disrespecting the Viceroy of Ecthelowall. He would tell me to accept your offer." Thomas chuckled softly. He could almost hear the exasperation in Hurstwell's voice over him.

Ecthelion tapped on the parchment but said nothing.

Swallowing, Thomas leaned forward, pulling the parchment to himself. He read it over, and over, and for a third time before he had nearly the whole of it seared into his memory for life. This would change the course of his life.

My King, you know I want this. Do you approve?

The answer wasn't as clear or magnificent as when he'd seen the High King in the vision months ago. Or even as sharp as the rebuke to his inattention to his studies as Knight while waiting in this room.

Clearing his throat, Thomas locked his gaze firmly on the Viceroy. "You honor, with all respect, there is one thing I must ask of you before I can give my answer."

"Go on," Ecthelion said his voice gilded with bemusement.

"I need a document drafted. A different one. One ... for ... well ..."

Ecthelion smiled broadly. "I think I can guess what you're wanting."

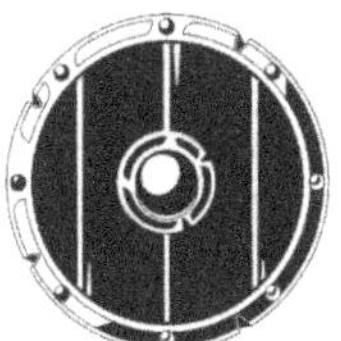

Thomas jogged up the last round of stairs to reach the turret which housed Mia's quarters. He had precious little time to see her before the battle began. It might have been much to hope Mia wouldn't be soured over him cutting their time together to only a few moments, even if it was to see the Viceroy.

Perhaps she would surprise him, though. Today had certainly been filled with them already. Reflexively, Thomas gripped tighter the folio he carried. Within was the document he requested, signed and sealed with the Viceroy's signet. There was no one to stop him from coming straight to Mia's door, which dampened his buoyant mood some.

"Where are you, Norvik? Only been hired for a couple of days and already absent from your duty?" The Dag Votere mercenary had been handpicked to assist him in his duties of protecting Mia after they had arrived at Dirkforge. He was about Thomas's size, but blond and hardened by the years in difference between them. On their first meeting, something about him reminded Thomas of his cousin Mark.

Rapping his knuckles on the thick panels of her of chamber door, he waited for several minutes without an audible response. By now, Ilsa should have been back with Mia as well and seen to answering the door. Though it would have to mean something was amiss, Thomas hoped Ilsa wasn't here. Their last encounter had been strange and left him with an unease he couldn't really explain.

Maybe she's in the infirmary visiting Gregor?

The door swung open just as Thomas was about to turn and walk away. There was Mia, curling red tresses falling over one shoulder and garbed in a loose-fitting evening dress. It was a rich green to match her eyes and silky, perhaps the nicest thing she owned. Not for public attire, of course, but something that added beauty and hope to this day. The expression she wore, however was far from beautiful, restful, or hopeful. Anger simmered in those emerald eyes. "I didn't think you were coming."

When she didn't move from the doorway to allow him to enter, he knew he was in serious trouble. He hadn't seen this kind of ire from her since before their fateful trip headed for Yerst Castle. "I'm sorry I'm late. The Viceroy wanted to see me."

Her hands went to her hips and she challenged, "Really? What could the Viceroy have wanted from you that took more than an hour?"

"What do you mean by that?" He didn't like the dismissiveness in her tone.

Mia crossed her arms over her chest and shot him a look that said he knew exactly what it meant. She was saying he wasn't worthy of meeting the Viceroy. He was a nobody.

The look and the verbal barb were so much more the mannerisms of the old Mia he knew, it drew Thomas up short.

Slicing through the swell of anger and shame they had induced in him.

Gentle as a late spring breeze, he replied, "You're right. I'm nothing special. But you've never treated me that way. What's going on, Mia?"

"You may refer to me as Baroness Sornfold. And you know exactly what's going on. Or did you think I wouldn't notice how you've been avoiding me since we were captured?"

"Oh," he replied dumbly. It shouldn't have surprised him that she was aware of the distance he'd been keeping, but he hadn't expected this kind of response.

"Yeah, 'Oh, I got caught,'" she replied in a tone that mocked his. "If you didn't have feelings for me, then why play at it? To torment me? You were never that cruel, even when we were children."

Once more, he felt himself bristling at her accusations. But he reined it in, knowing he had brought this on himself. "I haven't been playing at anything. I love you, Mia. So much so that I risked the future of our people trying to keep you safe at Kilkern's Redoubt and again when we were escaping your sister's camp. I could've gotten Gregor out, but not at the cost of you."

There was a twinge of something in the set of her lip. A wavering that told him she was at war within. Did she really think he had only pretended to care about her?

He reached out and took one of her hands in his. She jerked at his hold but not hard enough to break it.

Trying his best to erect breakers to the surging sea of feelings overwhelming him, Thomas fixed her with his most earnest gaze. He had two choices now. To wall up his heart completely and shut her out, sever their bond indefinitely and walk away. Or he could be open and honest. Brutally, embarrassingly honest. Knowing what was in his folio, he knew what he had to do.

"Mia. I know at one time we didn't see eye to eye, but I've grown to love you. Truly and deeply. I can't live without you. If I'm guilty of anything, it's being a coward and keeping my distance because I loathe the thought of watching you leave me behind when this war is over. Watching you fall in love with some noble and spend your life with him while I stand at guard outside your chambers."

"Thomas, no. I could never do that ..." Mia protested, but she trailed off. Her countenance shifted, hardening. She had been caught up in the moment and must have long ago figured out what he had about the eventuality of their relationship.

"You were putting distance between us to avoid breaking my heart?" Her tone took on a note of incredulity and rekindled ire.

"Yes," he admitted. "It was foolish and craven, but yes."

She jerked free her hand. "Well, you can have all the space you like. Go and enjoy it with Ilsa. Your services—" she hesitated, her eyes glimmering with tears she forbade to fall.

For an instant his heart teetered on the same precipice as her words. If she finished, "not required," it would mean she was dismissing him from her guard. More than that, he would lose not only any access to her, but his livelihood, his place in society. He would be a cast-off, and she knew that. If she finished that sentence, it would be as if she wished he didn't exist at all. From the societal station she held, that would effectively be the reality in which they each would live going forward.

She stared at him, her mouth still open. It was impossible to know what his face betrayed. This was so far from what he'd come to the tower expecting, from what he'd imagined, what he'd hoped—his chest felt shackled, unable to draw in a breath.

Mia closed her mouth and drew in a shaky breath. "Go. Now," she commanded through clenched teeth.

Part of him wanted to obey, to run from this horrible perversion of what their last moments before a battle that could claim his life should be. A battle he fought in large part to safeguard hers. Deep inside, he knew if he did, though, there would be no coming back. No second chance to make things right. "No," he asserted. "I can't leave while you're hurting like this."

"Ha! Then you shouldn't have started a courtship with my handmaiden."

Thomas gaped at her. "A relationship with your handmaiden ... you mean Ilsa?"

"Of course, I mean Ilsa," Mia replied, rolling her eyes. "I know you became close during our captivity."

"She's a Knight now, so I feel obligated to mentor her. But I haven't spent any time with her when you weren't there."

"Apart from when I sent her to retrieve you earlier?" Mia challenged. "And you're a fool for choosing her over me if you're doing it because you think she's a Knight like you."

Thomas shook his head as if that could clear the haze of confusion he was embroiled in. "Why would you think I'm trying to court Ilsa?"

Arms crossed over her chest, Mia's cheeks reddened, either from embarrassment or anger or both. "I'm not blind or deaf. I see the way she ogles you and talks endlessly about you as if you're Cinaed of Tislatna returned to flesh. And you're right, you aren't the only one aware that, at some point, society would have forced us apart. At least I had the courtesy not to snag the first alternative like some angler fishing off the pier!"

Thomas gaped at Mia for several seconds and drew in a calming breath. "Mia?"

"What?" Her voice harsh.

"You need to read what's in this folio. Right now."

She rolled her eyes. "Leave it on the table by the window, and I'll look at it if I—"

"Mia, read it! Now." Thomas raised his voice to her for the first time in their relationship.

The effect was as hoped. She was so startled by it that even in her anger and bitterness, she muttered, "Fine." She jerked it from his hands and tore off the wax seal without even seeing who had sealed it.

Her eyes scanned down the document quickly, and Thomas could tell the moment she read what he wanted her to see because her eyes went from dull with indifference to sharp, quickened. "Thomas, this is a contract proposing marriage to my House of Sornfold from the House of Halifax."

Letting out a sigh, Thomas nodded. "Mm-hmm."

"That's the Viceroy's family line."

"I know," he said, a little grin turning up the corner of his mouth as the faintest air of hope breezed into the space between them, fresh and ever so welcome.

"Why are you smiling?" she asked, confusion overriding her annoyance.

"Keep reading. The names of the intended are below."

Once more, he watched her eyes, knowing she would give it away before her training in guarding her emotions could mask it. Sure enough, her eyes widened dramatically, and he could tell she was re-reading it. Her gaze lifted to his, brows knitted in question. "The intended are Baroness Mia Sornfold and Sir Thomas Halifax?"

By now he was beaming a smile. He put his hands over hers and all but whispered, "Yes. I am guilty of foolishness regarding you, but nothing like disloyalty. On the contrary, maybe I'm too bound to you. Too enamored. Because when this war is over, I want to spend all the days remaining in my life by your side."

Thomas had never seen Mia's eyes so wide, so vulnerable. He could feel her hands shaking a little. His hold was gentle and he rubbed them with soft, soothing strokes of his thumbs.

"But you ..." She mumbled. "The Viceroy ..."

"That's why he wanted to see me," Thomas finished for her. "He offered to adopt me. To restore the honor and wholeness of both our families. The first request I made as his legal son was for him to draft this."

"I can't breathe." She sounded every bit as robbed of air as she claimed.

Spotting an upholstered sedan, Thomas helped her over and crouched down beside the couch, still holding her hands. He kept quiet, his smirk gone. By now, nothing should seem surprising so long as it wasn't what he expected. This most definitely wasn't what he had in mind for this moment.

After sitting in the chair, staring fixedly at the parchment in hand, Mia's breathing evened out, and she looked at him. Her expression, beyond shocked, was hard to read.

"Mia?" he inquired pitifully. "Are you okay?"

"Yes," she answered. "And no."

The Ameremare Sea was a smaller divide from what he envisioned and what was unfolding. "I'm sorry. I shouldn't have sprung this on you. I should have found a better way, a better time, but you came so close to casting me out of your life forev—"

"Thomas, stop talking."

He fell silent as instructed. Mia's cheeks were taut with tension, and her eyes held depths the Ameremare could never hope to reach. Depths he could fathom for a lifetime and not exhaust.

She stood, breaking his hold on her hands, and though she was a bit wobbly at first, Mia moved across the room with slow, sure steps. He might have imagined it, but it looked like she was biting one of her fingernails.

Thomas watched her, unable to move. Unsure if he should follow or leave or stay put. In the end, gravity, both natural and that which Mia exerted on him, kept him in place.

His gaze dropped to the smooth stone floor. Marble here, with swirls of grey amidst the white, twisting and turning in a dance of hues within a polished veneer that reflected the fast-passing afternoon sunlight. His thoughts turned back for the first time to the battle he must join. The curiosity of the Emeralans seemingly planning to attack so close to dusk had not yet sunk in for him. Not until this moment.

Fighting in unfamiliar fens after nightfall will be treacherous for them. They must know that. So why attack now?

As if his thoughts had prompted it, the strident notes of the ram's horn, calling him to the battle, echoed up into the tower. He had to leave right away. Get to his position. The horn meant the enemy had taken up its position. Soon they would attack.

Rising to stand, he saw Mia was hunched over the parchment, pushing something into it.

"There," she announced, striding over and handing him the parchment. "That's my answer."

Thomas was almost too afraid to look, but he dreaded more not knowing and so peered down at the sheet which weighed less than the shirt he wore but more than all the riches of Lowlands.

"Wait," Mia spoke up suddenly, her voice thready and cracking. "Don't read it yet."

Thomas's brows knit together. "What?"

"Not until the battle is over," she instructed, her expression becoming more schooled.

He shook his head, her expression was unreadable. What did it mean that she didn't want him to know her answer?

Barely above a whisper, and that carried with all the courage he could muster, he asked, "Why?"

She scowled at the floor tracing some of the swirls on the marble with her foot. Seconds stretched in silence before she admitted, "I don't want what it says to be what you're thinking about down there. No matter my answer, you focus on surviving the battle. Winning for our people. Then we can resolve," she swallowed hard, "us."

Her eyes finally lifted back to his, and his heart could scarce be more tempest-tossed. How was he supposed to breathe, much less fight a battle? The way she looked at him was with such caution, as though he were glass, and she dared not shift him the wrong way lest he shatter. Maybe it was reading too much into it, but she cared. No matter what she had decided about the proposal, she cared about him.

"All right," he said. "Not till after the battle is over." He tucked the parchment within his armor so that it sat over his heart. Knowing she cared was enough, for now.

17

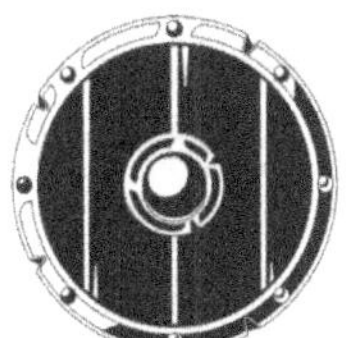

Sitting atop the horse provided for him, Thomas kept his eyes shut. Around him, the sounds of the Restoration Army's soldiers resounded off the stones of the castle walls. He could hear through the discordant sounds, the clopping of a horse's hooves near him though. Over his heart, the weight of the unopened parchment felt like a hot coal—no, an entire forge's furnace worth of the stuff.

"You know, any moment, they'll give the signal, and the gate will be opened. You will be forced to face your fear, lad," Kilkern informed him in a cool, sterile way.

Thomas drew in a breath, trying not to give into the annoyance he felt at Kilkern of all people giving him advice. In his distraction, he hadn't noticed the Steward had come up alongside him.

"I'm not afraid of the danger to myself from them." Thomas kept his eyes shut. Perhaps it would offput the Steward and he would join the other nobles in the back, where they had tried to move Thomas as well. Word had traveled fast that he was the new heir to House Halifax.

"Oh. I suppose then you fear something we cannot see?"

It annoyed him how perceptive the old physician could be. Under his breath, Thomas recited the words etched on his spiritsword, the pommel of which his hand gripped tightly.

"Or do you feel the High King will keep you safe amid the bloodshed?" Kilkern continued to prod.

Some of Thomas's apprehension eased. At least Kilkern didn't know all the dimensions of which Thomas's anxieties consisted. "My life belongs to him. If he favors me with safety and seeing victory, that is good. If I ride out for the last time and join him in the Highlands, that, too, is good."

That was what he was reminding himself as much as rebuffing the Steward. In the midst of the fray ahead, he could not think about Mia. About a future with her. It wasn't his to claim, as much as he wanted it and as close as he may be to reaching it.

"Aye, lad. Aye. Good that your thoughts are on the Highlands over the high towers here. Or anywhere in these Lowlands. My thoughts keep going to my son ..."

Thomas opened his eyes. Kilkern's admission startled him. The older man merely arched a brow and said, "We don't have the authority to say whom we shall preserve alive in this war. A hard lesson to learn. Better to keep your thoughts elsewhere. Hm?"

"Is there something you want, Steward?" Thomas was torn over whether the other man was trying to pick at his loyalty to the High King or praise it.

Kilkern gave a little shrug, which still looked like a dramatic gesture in his bulky armor. "It's dusk, and we're about to rush out against our enemy. Don't you find their strategy ... odd?"

"A bit," Thomas admitted.

"Good. While you're out there, make sure you stay alive to

figure out what is really going on. Mark my words, these Emeralans are craftier than this. There's something ..."

The horn sounded, ending the conversation.

"May the High King be with us," he murmured, reverently. Ahead, dozens of soldiers on foot rushed out into the twilight-garbed battlefield.

The soldiers of the defense spread out onto the field of battle, wave by wave. As Thomas passed under the gatehouse, he heard the twang of bows and crossbows from atop the walls. They were firing into the distance, forcing the enemy to hold back as Dirkforge's defenders rushed them.

Glancing behind, Thomas saw Kilkern had pulled back and was staying with the other nobles: Steward Malcolm of Dirkforge, Steward Prescot of the neighboring stewardship of Baileòrna, and Viceroy Ecthelion, the latter of whom gave a reassuring nod to Thomas.

Returning the nod, Thomas steeled himself and spurred his horse onto the darkened battlefield. At the periphery of the formations, soldiers carried swords and torches. Overhead, the first faint hint of stars was becoming visible as the sky deepened from lavender and mauve to indigo. Looking down on it all was one notable absence—the moon. It should have been out and visible by now but wasn't, and not for cover of clouds. It had been days since Thomas had checked on its phase, but he guessed it must be a new moon. Something about that tickled at the edges of his consciousness.

From his left, the third son of Steward Malcolm called out, "Cannons ahead, form up and flank them. We must remove them, or they'll shred through our ranks!"

Refocusing on the task at hand, Thomas followed the other mounted soldiers as they wheeled off from the main force as if in retreat and made a wide cut back around to come at the unmistakable line of heavy artillery field pieces. The maneuver was sloppy and obvious. They bore down on the artillery crews, and Thomas could see why no one had bothered to interrupt their attack and why the cannons and mortars weren't yet pounding the castle walls. The cannons were half sunken into the soft soil of the fen, and the crews were struggling to right them and get them into position. The small, mounted group tore through the artillery lines. The anticipated sounds of arquebusier guns firing never hindered them. A startling surprise, as from this range, they could easily have peppered the riders with enough fire to take down several of them.

Thomas almost crashed his steed into a cannoneer, peering into the lines of the Emeralans' ranged ranks. Some struggled with their weapons, clearly having difficulty with getting them to fire. Perhaps their powder got wet during their march here. It would certainly be possible, given a few recent rains that had passed through the area.

This is almost too easy. They have few, if any, conventional bowmen among them, and no siege equipment to take down the castle walls.

The Emeralans' sword and halberd-bearing ranks were holding their own against the soldiers for the Restoration, but it would hardly be enough to win the sort of victory they needed to advance deeper into Albaron's lands. If they were to be routed, then Caldoness could send its full army to intercept the Monarch's personal force and overwhelm him in the mountains. There was a good chance they could capture him and force an armistice, if not an outright surrender.

Could they really be on the edge of both victory and defeat? Were the Monarchists so arrogant that they completely bungled this offensive?

As if in response to the question, a keening horn called from the Emeralans' side, and their lines shattered as they turned and dashed in full retreat from the fen.

Kilkern's misgivings and Thomas's own unease made what he was seeing seem impossible. Though they could hardly have known how much the Monarchists would struggle with the terrain. It all seemed too easy. Too simple. Kilkern had warned him to think through what he saw out here. What if the Emeralans were playing them? Drawing them away from the castle for ... something else. But what?

"Hey, common stock," Malcolm's son called to him. "I know you're new to this, but when your commander orders you to pursue the enemy in a rout, you ride to rout!"

Shaking his head, Thomas replied. "I'm sorry ... it's just I don't think this all there is to—"

"Of course, you don't. You were just pulled from the ruts! You don't know a thing about any of this. So, shut up and follow ... or dash back to your new daddy and leave this battle to the true nobles."

So much for me helping to bring peace and balance. If the Ecthel nobles react this way, I might be the cause for a civil war instead of preventing one.

Though Thomas had seen more battles, and from all he'd observed, far better technique and fighting acumen than Malcolm's son, there was no point in arguing. Better he not become a point of contention and grievance for the Restoration's member factions.

"You're right," Thomas replied. "Forgive me, sir. I think it best if I do turn back."

The other rider's nose crinkled in disgust. "Do us all a favor. Quit playing noble. You're clearly not suited for its demands of honor and intellect."

With that, he wheeled around his steed and spurred it on in chase of the retreating Emeralans. Soon everyone had disappeared into the distance and dark. Thomas sat on his steed, trying not to care what had been said to him, but found the words impossible to avoid. Perhaps Steward Malcolm's son was right. He didn't fit that life anymore. Maybe he would only bring strife by becoming Ecthelion's heir.

A flush of movement at the periphery of his vision jerked him out of his inner turmoil. At the edge of the battlefield, something rather large and very fast dashed across the fen toward the castle walls.

Another mysterious blur and another streaked by. A fourth sped past, this time so close he felt a faint and torrid wind off the thing. His heart thudded in his chest. This was not the first time he had seen such things. Anargen had related an old children's rhyme to him after the battle in Kirke:

"Dread fangs in the night,
Fear at its height.
New moon's gain,
Full moon's bane."

"Werebeasts," he muttered under his breath.

Was that their game? Lure as many of the Restoration forces away as possible and then let these wretched monsters wreak havoc? But there must have been some mistake. Surely there were nowhere near enough to take down the entire fortress and city—not before the army returned. At least if there were enough Knights of Light present, the foes would fail.

He was missing something. Something important, and he couldn't quite place it. If they couldn't take the castle outright, then what were they planning? At Kirke one of their kind had snuck into the city to attempt ...

Thomas gasped.

Of course. They tried to assassinate Viscount Geralian in Kirke. Now they're here to kill the Viceroy!

Worse, they could be after them all. Mia, Gregor, the Stewards. How would the war effort recover from that? Even if the whole Restoration didn't founder, the infighting Ecthelion feared would be tenfold and destroy any chance of peace for generations.

Peering into the dark to where the others had disappeared, Thomas wavered. It would be risky to try to stop all of them without help.

They wouldn't take me seriously. May the High King help me, Ecthelowall stands or falls tonight.

He drew in a breath and gripped his spiritsword. Its warmth coursed up his arm, and he knew the High King's favor was on him, whatever lay ahead. Thomas yelled, "Hi-yah!" and spurred his horse toward the fortress and the fate of his people.

18

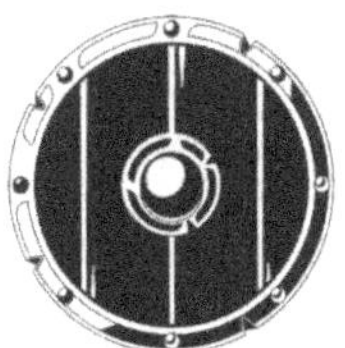

"Faster!" he pleaded with his horse, dreading they weren't swift enough. By the time he reached the gatehouse, he could see the beasts weren't opting for subtlety. The portcullis was smashed, its iron mesh a twisted ruin. By the light of the torches along the wall, he spotted two of the fiends perched on either side of the gatehouse, battering aside bowmen and arquebusiers as if they were mere pests. Mosquitoes buzzing in their ears and nothing more.

The other two must have already advanced deeper into Dirkforge. As Thomas crossed under the gatehouse at a gallop, part of him demanded he keep riding. His hands, his heart ached to hold Mia, to shelter her from the evil falling upon the fortress.

Even stronger was the sting of his memory of every time he had failed to show compassion for others. In honesty, acting primarily in consideration of his desires and not the nation's, as he had told himself. If he opened himself to it, he knew the High King was directing him to turn aside and aid the soldiers on the walls. Their deaths would be tragedies, just as any others.

Veering across a particularly soggy patch of the fens, he cut toward the nearest stairs up onto the wall. He barely slowed as he reached it. Leaping off his horse, he grabbed hold of the first landing and pulled himself up. Up and up, he dashed until, panting, he was on the wall, thirty feet higher than where he started. He looked down the wall segment to where an Albaron bowman had drawn a long knife and tried to slash one of the beasts.

His lycanthropic opponent merely cocked its head to the side and barked out a wolfish laugh. IIt grabbed the man and smashed him into the parapet. The archer's light chest plate made a crunching sound as he crumpled and slid down the stone defensive works. Like a feline bored with its mouse, the thing lifted the archer up and batted him over the parapets without another glance.

Thomas drew his spiritsword and raised his shield. Fire caught on both, burning along their inscriptions bright enough to catch the eye of the creature, even from more than a dozen yards away.

The young Knight took one step toward the monster, and a rush of heat encircled him. It held him back from advancing.

Seeing his hesitation, the werebeast narrowed its ochre eyes and stalked forward on its hind legs. It, like all the others of its kind Thomas had seen, looked like a wolf, a man, a bear, and a boar had been united into one creature. He knew its powerful limbs and sharp claws could rend stone, but it had the mind and malice of man.

Hackles raised, the beast issued a low growl and surged forward, bounding toward him on all fours. The creature closed the distance in seconds, landing a few feet away and throwing itself at him, ravenous jaws snapping.

A familiar whisper reached Thomas's ear. It turned the warmth to fire within him.

Not wasting an instant, Thomas lunged, gripping his spiritsword and launching straight past the snapping jaws to hammer his sword in deep.

One stunned eye on the creature widened, flames reflected in it from the spiritsword as Thomas jerked it free from the beast's now sizzling wound. Smoke from the strike made it cough as it staggered back a step and stumbled over the parapet, dropping down to where it had thrown the Albaron moments before.

Drawing in a steadying breath, Thomas pushed past the pang in his chest for the loss of both. Inside that horrible creature had been a person. A man twisted and poisoned by darkness and beguiled by its sorceries. Lost to it like Delia had become. Who out there even now missed the man within the monster?

He shook his head to clear. There was no good in lingering on such things now. On the other wall section was another fiend as foul as the first, wantonly tearing through the Ecthel and Albaron soldiers feebly defending it.

Without a second's more hesitation, he sprinted with divinely aided speed. He scaled the damaged upper portions of the gatehouse, agilely navigating the narrow ledges and handholds needed to reach the other side. From atop the other side, he peered down at the second creature several yards away. It bore down on a soldier who lay sprawled and injured on the wall.

Feeling the flush of heat from his blade, Thomas jumped over to land in front of the werebeast. His heart thrummed both from the exertion and shock of what had just happened. Even if he'd experienced the wonders of the High King's favor before, it was no less astonishing to him.

A bowman scrambled behind Thomas to help pull away the prone man. A low growl issued from the werebeast's muzzle. Fangs bared, its hot, fetid breath created little misty swirls in the night air.

Mia's face flashed before him, stoic but only just, an immense pain simmering within. Surely someone in the Lowlands felt the same about the being before him.

"I won't allow you to harm anyone else," Thomas informed the creature. He was careful to keep ready, tensed to react. "But it doesn't have to come to that. Your fellow beast fell because it rejected the High King's rule. There is no reason you need to err—"

The creature shuddered and bellowed out something akin to a roar. It flung itself at Thomas. Crashing into his fiery shield, its fur was instantly singed, but it ignored the pain. Swiping huge, clawed forepaws at Thomas, it failed to land a blow.

Roaring again, it reached around the shield with one clawed hand while the other gripped it to prevent it from being moved to block.

One slash connected with Thomas's helmet with a forceful hit that would have laid him open from top of his head to the jaw if he weren't so well armored. Spots floated in Thomas's vision, partially obscuring the beast.

Ironically, the creature's hold on his shield kept Thomas from falling backward. He regrouped in time to bring his fiery sword around in an arc, deterring another slash and scoring a shallow graze along the beast's hand and forearm. The monster jerked away and Thomas stepped into the space, cracking it on the head with his shield.

He jumped over a low swipe the creature attempted and brought down his spiritsword in a slice across its right shoulder, leaving a searing, glowing laceration.

The monster cried out in pain and fell back, trying to scramble away.

"You don't have to be destroyed," he insisted. "The High King's light can dispel the gloom entrapping—"

Barking in rage, the creature ripped free a parapet stone from the wall and flung it at Thomas.

The teen dropped to the ground as the stone crashed and shattered into fragments behind him.

Okay, that's a definite no.

Clenching his teeth, Thomas blocked right to deflect the monster's claws as it raked them across his shield again, hungry to do so to his flesh. He dodged left and leaped onto the parapet stones facing the castle interior. The creature looked up at him, surprise and hatred in the curl of its canid lips. It barked and pawed at him.

Thomas jumped over the sloppy attack and landed on its enormous back, plunging the burning blade in deep. Holding on tight, he didn't let the fiend shake him off until it collapsed forward.

Pulling free the spiritsword, he jumped off and turned to look back on the smoking ruin of the beast.

"Ugh." Now that he wasn't focused on fighting, he realized how much his head hurt. His foe had been determined to end him and very nearly succeeded.

A horn sounded in the distance—Albaron's army was in retreat. That couldn't be. They had overwhelmed the Monarchists.

No. No. No! There must have been a trap laid beyond the fens.

More werebeasts—or worse. Whatever it was, he could not linger here in wait. He had to stop the two other monsters. If he was favored to live and succeed at that task, then he could return to help shore up the defenses.

An odd feeling overtook Thomas, and he realized he was being watched by several of the surviving wall defenders. To the nearest of them, he addressed, "You heard the horn?"

"Yes, sir," one replied, clearing his throat.

"You'll need to hold this wall against whatever routed our forces. I must go after the other two of their kind that entered the fortress."

"Other two, sir?" another man said. "I only saw three of their kind attack the gatehouse."

The others were quick to agree. "Yes, it was three. I'll never in my life forget those fangs and their horrid stench."

"That complicates things," Thomas mused. "I distinctly saw four of them dashing across the fens to attack the castle."

"I saw a hooded figure slip in just after the attack began," the first guard volunteered. "At least, I think that's what I saw. It didn't make sense. Whoever or whatever they are took off toward the western battlements.

All of Thomas's muscles tensed. "They're trying to use the secret causeway along it to get into the interior of the keep."

"Ha, foolish mongrels," one of the arquebusiers chuffed. "The Viceroy and Stewards aren't in there. They're in the courtyard."

That is true, and from the battlements, he would have to have seen that to be the case. There's something else to this ...

"Oh, no," Thomas muttered. Anxiety surged within him. The Stewards and Viceroy weren't the hooded attacker's targets. "He's after the Baroness and Heir Apparent!"

A look passed among the Albarons that Thomas knew meant their concerns were still alleviated. So, he fixed a pointed stare on those wearing Ecthel green. "I need a detachment of your best men to check and make sure that both the Baroness and Heir Apparent are safe while I go after the remaining werebeast. Can you handle that?"

"Yes, sir," an older Ecthel leaning against his halberd answered, straightening. He motioned to a trio of other soldiers. "Get Frederick and Nathan. Bring them to meet me at the west tower. Be quick about it."

While the trio bustled off, the older man whom Thomas now recognized to be Sergeant Strathmore, a seasoned veteran from the recapture of Port Valence on, faced him again. "Sir Fenwrest, word of your skill precedes you, and by all accounts, was fully earned. I bid you caution in your pursuit of those foul creatures. But uh ... well, do you have any counsel as to what we shall face?"

Thomas frowned. "I didn't see the being that was described. If they transformed from werebeast to man again under a full moon's watch, then even from what little I know of them makes that particular beast extremely potent and, therefore, all the more dangerous. I wouldn't suspect they would send only a single werebeast to face down the Viceroy and Stewards, though, so this person is likely something ... else."

Strathmore twitched his bristly gray mustache. "I understand. We shall give our all for the Golden Forest. Hale evening, ever before the dawn of Ecthelowall's Commonwealth."

"Hale evening, ever before the dawn of Ecthelowall's Commonwealth."

A thought struck Thomas as the other man turned to leave. If the sentry was right, and some fiend of unknown prowess and terrors had gone after Mia and Gregor, it was likely the group would only be able to save one. Though it would destroy him personally, he knew which one they had to safeguard to most assure Ecthelowall's survival.

Gnawing at his lip, Thomas broke and called to Strathmore. "When you're going to secure the keep, it will be faster if you collect the Baroness first, but the Heir Apparent is in more dire need of aid."

The aged Sergeant nodded slowly. "I catch your meaning, sir. The boy will be our priority."

Hearing the words aloud, even if he encouraged them, almost took Thomas's legs out from under him. Under his breath, he begged, "Please, my Great King, keep them all safe. Deliver them over me."

Thomas knew that was not how the High King worked. He couldn't trade himself for them. Nor was the High King limited to only saving one group or the other. Both hinged on his favor, and both may be in his will to rescue or neither. Yielding to that knowledge was so very, very hard. Even with understanding, the Great King's wisdom far exceeded his as much and more so than the Highlands where he reigned from towered over the Lowlands. Eager to do all his part in the matter, he forced more speed out of his legs as he dashed down the stairs from the wall and toward the inner courtyard from which echoed a wicked, glee-filled howl.

19

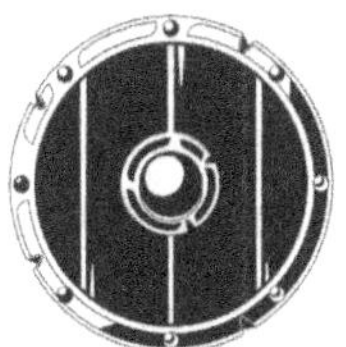

Bounding across the last bridge over the fen between the outer curtain wall and the interior wall, Thomas barely slowed. A smoky haze hung in the air. All the torches and lanterns from the gatehouse into the paved stone courtyard beyond had been snuffed out and smoldered. In the dark, it evoked the sensation of a long burned-out hearth fire. Worse, a spent funeral pyre.

As he passed under the open gatehouse to the courtyard, he noticed this one wasn't shattered. At least its stones remained intact. The comparison to the pyre was tragically appropriate, however, for the guards whose bodies floated in the moat on either side of the bridge. Up on the walls, the crossbowmen and arquebusiers were oddly silent. Once Thomas entered the courtyard, he understood why. In the center of the courtyard, the monster circled and snapped at a pair of figures, swords raised in guard. One sword burned brightly, a beacon in the diminished light. Viceroy Ecthelion.

At his side was someone else—Steward Malcolm. Around them was the carnage of all the noblemen's' felled bodyguards.

To the far periphery, Thomas could make out Steward Kilkern crouched over the body of another Steward. Practicing his physician's arts, noticeably checking on the progress of the battle periodically.

Whispers reached Thomas's ears from those on the wall. They were unable to fire for risk of hitting the nobles and too frightened to climb down and aid the rulers, having seen how mortally dangerous the werebeast could be.

A low, feral growl issued from the creature. It had noticed Thomas's slowed approach. When he held his spiritsword at the ready and advanced with his shield up in guard, the beast narrowed its eyes and bared its dripping fangs.

He was still a dozen paces back, but upon the creature's distraction, Ecthelion and his ally sprang and charged it, attacking from each side.

An instant before the blades could land, its pointed ears twitched, and it leaped up and forward, landing a few feet away from the pair of nobles. In a blur of coarse brown fur, it bore down on the Steward to its left, bashing him with a hand balled into a fist that sent Malcolm to his knees with a cry of pain. The thing narrowly avoided a follow-up from the Viceroy, the tufts of fur around its neck singed by the nearness of Ecthelion's spiritsword.

It reared back and barked a warning at the Viceroy, swiping with its despicably sharp claws and rending the air with an audible *whoosh* where the Viceroy's head had just been.

By now, Thomas was near enough to put pressure on the creature and force it back. Though he couldn't back it too far. Steward Kilkern was several feet away in that direction, clearly working feverishly over the contused and bloodied body of the other Steward, who must be Prescot. Thomas couldn't see who it was that Kilkern was working on, but it had to be Prescot since Thomas couldn't spot him anywhere else in the courtyard. If he pushed the monster too much, the beast might notice the two vulnerable rulers and opt to cut its losses and inflict the greatest damage it could before retreating.

To Thomas's surprise, the creature stood its ground and even wore an evil perversion of a doggish grin, its thick reddened tongue lolling out of one side of its mouth as it barked a laugh. It turned its head away toward Steward Kilkern and yapped something.

Before Thomas could act on it, Ecthelion seized on the advantage and sprang at the werebeast from behind.

The monster seemed to know he was coming and ducked low, under Ecthelion's blade's swipe. It surged up and backhanded Ecthelion, sending him flying to land hard on the stone several feet away.

"Viceroy!" Thomas shouted, knowing Ecthelion had opted not to wear Knightly armor and instead the more formal and societally dictated dress of his station to the battle. He wasn't supposed to be a combatant and certainly not against a foe like this.

Thomas surged forward, but the creature was already on Ecthelion. Rearing its head back, it snapped forward and sank its teeth into his shoulder.

"*No!*" Thomas screamed. He closed the remaining space in strides faster and longer than any in his life. He jumped onto the creature's back and slammed his spiritsword down into its hulking arched back.

It let out a horrific scream and released the Viceroy. Both clawed paw-like hands scratched wildly at Thomas, forcing him to pull loose his blade and drop to the ground with a roll.

An instant later, Thomas was on his feet again, his sword and shield readied. Smoke roiled off the creature's charred fur, and it staggered under the wound. Still, it wasn't down. Its size and ferocity in the face of such an injury told Thomas this was an older, more devoutly dark beast. Nothing but hatred and fury were in its eyes. All semblance of humanity was lost in those ochre depths. Its reddened jaws gaped open, ravenous, only to be sated by his demise.

From the ground, there was a flash of brilliance, and the creature let out a choked gasp. Ecthelion flung himself upward and drove his spiritsword into the monster's exposed underbelly.

Ecthelion collapsed onto the pavement with a groan, unable to hold onto the sword. He lay still, so very, very still.

"Viceroy," Thomas murmured. But he couldn't go to him. With his last bit of strength, Ecthelion had delivered a blow the creature couldn't recover from. It thrashed and wailed, a mad vortex of burning fur and fury. It was one of the most terrible and tragic things Thomas had ever seen.

He did his best to keep the creature from staggering into any of the wounded. No matter how painful it was to watch, he didn't take his eyes off the fiend until it dropped about five steps away from Ecthelion and went limp.

In the silence after, every breath, every beat of Thomas's heart felt thunderous, like it would echo off the Albar Mountains and back to him. He hoped with every fiber of his being never to witness anything like that again.

"Thomas," Ecthelion groaned.

The Viceroy's voice was so strained that it wrenched Thomas from his stupor and slammed him back to the stones of Dirkforge with devastating force. He collapsed onto his knees beside Ecthelion and lifted his faceplate. "Sir, I'm here. I'm so sorry, I should have come faster, I should have—"

Ecthelion put his hand over Thomas's mouth. The act was so shockingly without diplomacy that it completely silenced Thomas's spiraling, bumbling apology even within his thoughts.

"You did not cause this. But you must salvage the day. What is the state of things outside the walls?"

"Um, well ..." Thomas swallowed back a gulp of anxiety. The thin armor Ecthelion had worn was largely decorative and looked like a Jhiish porcelain dish that had been dropped. "The Emeralans fled but must have regrouped. Our army sounded a horn of retreat."

Ecthelion sucked in a sharp, belabored breath. "Then get Mia and Gregor out of here. Take as many warriors as will follow and make for Caldoness. They have to be warned ..." Another wave of pain contorted Ecthelion's thin face into a grimace that sent a jolt of discomfort through Thomas.

"Sir, we might be able to rally and—"

Once more, Ecthelion tried the hand trick, but Thomas caught it and gripped it tight. "And if I retreat, I'm not leaving you ... father."

"Warn them ..." Ecthelion jerked his hand free and with surprising force and violence gripped Thomas's face, forcing him to look the other direction. There, Steward Kilkern stood over Steward Malcolm's body, a long dirk drawn and poised to plunge downward into the unconscious noble.

Eyes widening with horror, Thomas shouted, "Kilkern, no! What are you doing?"

Tilting his head at an odd angle, Kilkern faced Thomas. In a voice that had the coarse vulgarity of the grave, he replied, "Aiding Steward Malcolm's trip to join Steward Kilkern."

He plunged the dirk down into Malcolm's chest with a sickening sound. Malcolm jerked to consciousness, moaned, and went limp again.

Thomas was on his feet, his grip tightening on his spiritsword. "Traitor!" he shouted, the accusation a furious maelstrom of shame and bitterness. Why had he trusted this snake twice now, only to be bitten so venomously? "You're why the retreat was sounded. Your troops turned on us in the middle of the battle, didn't they?"

Slowly, Kilkern stood and strode toward Thomas, dagger held casually at his side. "You're partially right, phosphila. My troops did surprise your army, but I was never on your side, and so am no traitor."

The voice was so unnerving, it had only the barest threads tethering it to the timbre and tone of Kilkern's. Something was off, and it went far beyond a simple betrayal.

"Kilkern, don't come any closer, or I will strike you down."

"Very well," Kilkern replied with a smirk, which twisted and bent until it along with Kilkern's whole face was no longer his own. In fact, his whole body seemed to now be that of Steward Prescot's.

Thomas gasped. What in the Lowlands was he seeing? Had that really just happened?

"Wh-what are you?" he stammered, backing away a few steps and raising his sword.

The thing sneered at the flush of heat and light reaching it from the blade. "It would be pointless to tell you. All that matters is that Steward Kilkern perished tonight." He gestured to the body Thomas had first seen Kilkern crouched over.

Looking intently, Thomas felt bile rise in his throat. It was Kilkern. Wide-eyed with horror, he stared at the thing before him.

It grinned, smarmy, and continued, "Prescot never made it, unfortunately, but I got to play his part and bring your miserable Restoration to this very moment." He clucked his tongue with great relish, "Devastation."

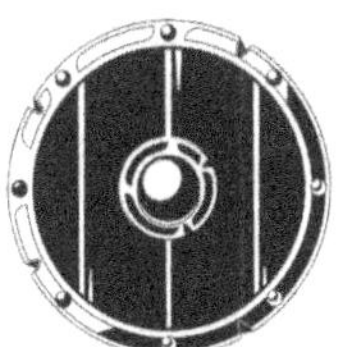

A horn blew from nearby. The retreat was drawing near. Calls echoed in the inner courtyard for the gates to be closed after the returning soldiers. They had no idea that the outer gatehouse had been destroyed, impossible to shut.

Thomas felt dizzy. This couldn't be happening. An hour ago, he was thinking about how close the Restoration was to a decisive victory. How could it all have fallen apart this way?

Oblivious to his crisis, or perhaps disturbingly cognizant of it, the changeling creature continued. "The Restoration is finished, and with Dirkforge's weapons and Baileòrna's food supplies lost. Albaron will fall with it. You won't live to see it, of course, but the Queen will be escorting the two usurpers you care so dearly for to Wyvares to witness the beginning of a new era for Ecthelowall and all of the Lowlands."

"That hooded figure. They're going to free Delia," Thomas muttered aloud, trying to hold himself steady and order his thoughts to keep grounded. He was faintly aware that the menacing Prescot lookalike was still slowly advancing and raising the dirk in its hand little by little with each step.

"Of course. This was the plan all along. You've made this so much easier for us to tend to those most precious to your cause." It gestured to the side with its free hand. "Viceroy Ecthelion will be dead soon. Malcolm may best him in reaching the grave. Steward Kilkern certainly has."

This isn't happening. This can't be real.

The creature stood right beside him.

It was too awful to be real. But no nightmare unfolded with such languid finality, such irrepressible weight bearing down on him.

"That's good. Just hold still little phosphila,a and your pain will be over so much swifter than the others ..."

Thomas felt so very tired. Ready to accept what came next. The teen's eyes flicked up to see the dirk poised over him, raised for a killing blow. All he had to do was heed the creature's words, and all of the pain and failure and devastation would end. Everything would end.

No!

Thomas tasted bile as disgust welled up within him at the idea of surrendering and forsaking his oaths. Those to defend Ecthelowall, the true Ecthelowall. Those he wanted to make to Mia, in love. Most of all, those he'd made to the High King.

His spiritsword flared with renewed fire and crackled as he stepped back and brought it around catching the creature across its chest. For an instant, the thing just stood there with Steward Prescot's eyes and expression, looking utterly stunned.

The reprieve was short, because even as the smoke rolled off the long, glowing wound, the creature unleashed a torrent of curses and expletives. These rose in frequency and pitch until it dropped to its knees, unable to resist the fire that seared to its core. As it collapsed, its face and shape transformed again. Whatever the creature was in its truest state, it was wholly indistinct. Average height and build, but with a face totally devoid of anything but a horrible blankness.

If pity would come for this cruel shapeshifter, it was too slow for Thomas to wait. He had to get to Mia and Gregor right away. But he couldn't, the army would need every capable soldier at the ready to repel the coming onslaught.

Wait. What about the Viceroy?

Thomas's gaze slipped back to Ecthelion lying some distance away from him. Thomas had only been the man's son for a few hours, and already he had forgotten his duty to him. No matter which way he turned, no matter which path he chose, people were going to die, and the Restoration could ill afford to lose any of them.

"Thomas?" Ecthelion reached out with his hand, which had been pressed against his mangled shoulder.

Dutifully, Thomas heeded the call, though the closer he got, the more anxiety pressed down on him. He crouched beside Ecthelion, taking his outstretched hand. The Viceroy's grip was weak, and his face was pale. "Yes, sir. I'm here."

Ecthelion nodded and then drew in a deep breath and fixed his gaze on Thomas. "Go. I heard what the doppelganger said. You must get to Mia and Gregor and stop Mia's sister."

Thomas shook his head, this was the direction he needed, but it felt so wrong to leave Ecthelion like this. "The army will need me. Kilkern's ... er ... the doppelganger's army and the Emeralans are going to bear down on us. It will be a terrible fight."

A grimace contorted Ecthelion's face for an instant, before he managed to get hold of himself again. "The lines will hold. Let the common soldiers battle common soldiers. You are one of the few Knights of Light we have, and Mia's sister is clearly ensconced in darkness. That darkness must not prevail. Do you understand me?"

Thomas gnawed on his lip for a moment. Another horn, rallying the lines for battle echoed into the courtyard. What if there was some new horror waiting just beyond the walls?

"Thomas," Ecthelion said, forcefully. "Son."

That grabbed Thomas's attention and pulled it squarely to the Viceroy. Seeing it effective Ecthelion continued, "I will endure. Our army will endure." He nodded to behind Thomas, where already a group of soldiers and the castle physicians were rushing toward them.

"Go. Now," Ecthelion reiterated.

Closing his eyes and steadying himself, Thomas shuddered as he waded through the mire of guilt and worry and fear to the shores of resolve Ecthelion was demanding of him. "Yes ... father."

A thin smile graced Ecthelion's lips. "Good. One thing, before you go. What was Mia's answer?"

Sharp and deep a twang of pain struck Thomas in his core and he instinctively reached for the letter, still tucked safely by his heart. "I ... I don't know. She wrote an answer but wouldn't let me read it till the battle is decided."

The Viceroy's smile broadened. "All the more reason to hurry then. Save her and the Restoration. Go."

Rising to his feet with the weight of reluctance pulling him down, Thomas took a few steps and looked back.

The Viceroy nodded to him to leave as the first physician reached him. "May the High King's favor be on you," Ecthelion called out, before others crowded around the Viceroy and blocked Thomas's view. All he could hear was hushed chattering, spoken too fast and too low to know his father's prognosis.

Thomas stared numbly at the scene for a few precious moments and backed away. At the edge of the courtyard's bounds, he turned and ran as fast as his armored boots endowed with the High King's blessing could carry him. As he slipped into the keep, he heard the cannon emplacements on the walls thundering. His fellow defenders were fighting back with all they had, just as Ecthelion said they would. Just as he must now.

At the first junction in the corridors of the keep, Thomas stopped. He closed his eyes and readied himself. "My Great King, whatever is ahead, I want to honor my oaths to you. Please, reveal the way forward."

There was no sudden flaming vision overhead to direct his path or elven messenger to deliver the guidance, but for the first time that night, perhaps in a long time, Thomas felt genuine peace come upon him. His mind found freedom from encumbrance, as though the sun had finally banished the heavy fog from lands he walked. Earlier, he had sent the group of defenders to collect Gregor, but if Delia had orchestrated all of this from the start, there was no doubt she would first have had her minion free her, and then ...

Mia.

Like the crack of the cannons outside, he launched himself headlong down the passageway leading up to Mia's quarters. He rounded the stairs of each floor in the tower she was housed in with barely a breath spent at each level. As he burst out onto the hall leading to her room, he was treated to exactly what he'd expected to find. The door was ripped from its hinges and lay shattered on the floor. Beyond the doorframe, he could see Delia flanked by her hooded minion. She had her eyes trained balefully on someone in a portion of the room Thomas could not see from the corridor. Mia must be there, defiantly returning that gaze and somehow holding her sister at bay.

Without hesitating, Thomas charged into the room and barreled straight into the hooded figure, sending them toppling to the ground beside the wall near the north-facing window.

This earned a slow, grudging turn of Delia's attention from Mia, whom Thomas could see was positioned toward the western end of the room, a sword in hand. He hadn't even realized she had one, though he couldn't spare the attention to get a good look at it. Not when he could feel the icy intensity of Delia's ire falling on him.

"Sir Fenwrest, this is a surprise," Delia commented. "I expected you to be busied with your duties elsewhere. Dogs aren't often let off their leashes in Albaron." Then as if a delicious thought occurred to her, the scowl she wore morphed into a cruel smile. "Or have my pets left you without a master?"

"I have *one* master—the High King of All Realms," Thomas replied, his tone level and his demeanor hard as stone. "He is your rightful master, too, whether you yield to that truth or not."

Delia's expression faded from pleasure to disgust. "I serve no man. Not in the Lowlands and certainly not in some myth-bound castle of the Highlands." Turning her attention ever so slightly toward Mia, she continued, "It seems your foolhardy convictions have fertile soil in my naïve little sister. She fancies herself a knight like you."

Incautious, his head whipped to take in Mia. She was standing in a guard stance he had taught her, both hands gripped tight enough to whiten her knuckles around the hilt of a broad spiritsword. At a glance, he knew two things that caught him by surprise. The first, that it was Sir Hurstwell's, and the second, it was not burning as he expected to see from Delia's comment. Which meant Mia was not, in fact, a Knight of Light. She had merely grabbed the spiritsword as opportunity and need dictated.

Even so, for the briefest moment, her eyes met his, and he saw in them a flicker of hope and warmth. Like a candle wick snuffed out by a strong breeze, however, Mia's expression fell deep into a pall of fear.

"Thomas, watch—" she cried out.

He turned to face an incoming attack an instant too late to ready a solid block and was sent reeling. The hooded attacker had regained its footing and held a black axe.

Staggering backward into a wall, Thomas just managed to get his shield up to block a second and third furious attack.

There was a startling intensity behind the strikes, but not finesse. Taking the fourth blow, Thomas glanced it off to the side and stepped forward into a jab with his fist to the hooded attacker's face. Stumbling backward, their hood fell back as well.

"Ilsa?" he asked, incredulity like thick cords around his throat, choking him.

She licked away the blood from a little split in her lip. There was a certain satisfaction in her expression. "Yes, Thomas?"

If under the hood had been an awful headlessness or a gorgon or any other manner of bizarre and monstrous creature, it could not have twisted his insides into any deeper knots of horror and revulsion. Words failed him.

Just out of sight, Delia clapped and deigned to snort and giggle like she'd seen a worthy comedy at Avon-caroon's renowned theater. "Oh, this is a treat," she said. "Has the mighty wielder of fire and light failed to uncover the truth? Shocking."

Her tone switched from amusement to one of mocking. "Perhaps not so shocking. Ilsa is among the most adept adherents to the arts of Tislatna's witches. Making others see what she wishes is her very nature. Would you care to know what the other is?

"Eviscerating those foolish enough to stand against me."

As if by command, Ilsa screeched a battle cry and crashed her black hand axe down on him with lethal precision. Thomas blocked, but was again on the defensive, and this time, Ilsa was more thoughtful about her strikes.

Amid the attacks, Delia called, "Now that my servant is attending to yours, little sister, we can conclude our business here."

There was a palpable fury in Mia's shout as she came at Delia. To his great distress, Thomas could not spare a moment's attention to aid her. If not for every evidence that Delia was fully imbued with dark powers, Thomas would have given Mia the fight on any day. But Delia had powers for which Mia was not properly guarded nor suited to combat. And if the servant so beset him, an aptly trained Knight, what evils could the mistress inflict?

He looked past Ilsa, needing to have his eyes on Mia as if it were enough to safeguard her. With her first swing she managed to set Delia back a step, but her older sister had produced a thin black blade by dark craft and was snapping out a black tether, no, a whip. Delia flicked her wrist and the dark whip cracked out and wrapped around Mia's waist. She jerked it sending Mia spiraling to the floor. Hurstwell's spiritsword clattered along the stone, away from her hands.

"Mia!" he called out.

"Eyes on me, phosphila," Ilsa taunted, her axe blow sending him spiraling around and nearly exposing his back to her next attack. "I'm the last woman you will see in these Lowlands. Besides, I'm sure the Baroness has no interest in you, not after I hinted to her how infatuated you are with me."

A growl issued from Thomas's chest, and he surged forward, taking an angry swipe at Ilsa that she easily dodged. "Lies! How did I not see you for the serpent you are?"

Ilsa knocked aside his next sloppy strike. A smirk tugged at her pale lips. In her free palms, dark mist gathered. A whip suddenly materialized. It was barbed with pointed hooks that were reminiscent of serpent fangs.

Thomas blocked its first strike with his shield, but that set his stance off. Ilsa didn't let up. Taking advantage of his faulty balance, she twirled into an attack with her axe.

The impact almost slammed him to the floor. A thrill of fear coursed through him. If he went down, he knew he wasn't getting up.

"It's as Queen Delia said. You see what I permit you to see. Nothing more. However, I did anticipate a greater challenge facing the knight who undid Thelxipeia's binding. To think I once envied my sister being selected as Oracle of Tislatna, and now I shall have the pleasure of killing the one who bested her."

The bizarre connection between the young woman who had been possessed by a goblin on the Isle of Geists—the same goblin who had, by Thelxipeia's hand, mortally wounded Sir Hurstwell—threw Thomas further off balance. He had to get space between them to process it all, at least as much as he could for now. Fending off another axe strike, he gauged that he could not do that physically now.

"You mean Poisella? We set her free."

As hoped, Ilsa lost her composure for a moment and blundered into his block, nearly getting caught by a quick counter from him. His verbal riposte had worked better than expected. She wasn't the only one with *unsettling* knowledge. "Yes, I know your sister's real name. And I know that she longed to escape the darkness that had imprisoned and consumed her."

Thomas could not say what had befallen the woman in the end, but he didn't need to. Ilsa backed away now, shaking her head and muttering curses. The distance gave him a moment to collect himself.

All of which was immediately undone as he looked to see Delia dragging Mia's unconscious body over to the window. She caught his eye and smirked, "Don't worry, Sir Fenwrest. I won't drop her here. She's needed in Wyvares."

To Ilsa, she instructed, "Grab the little pig after you finish him. No need to be gentle with either of them."

With that, she ducked out the window and flared her arms. From them unfurled membranous wings, akin to a bat's. Delia's feet took on the arched and taloned nature of a raptor's. With her bird-like claws, she gripped Mia by the shoulders and launched out into the night.

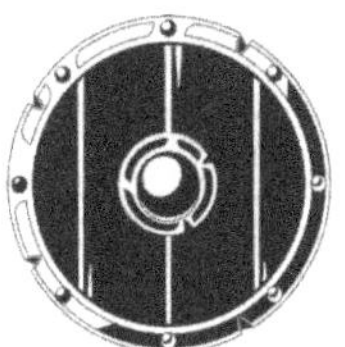

21

Had Thomas not seen many bizarre and awful things since becoming a Knight of Light, just the sight of Mia being carried off would have been enough to undo him. His heart felt like it had been frozen and then slammed mercilessly, shattered on the stone floor.

"You heard the Queen," Ilsa commented matter-of-factly. "You first. Then the boy." She snapped her wrist and struck at him with the barbed whip.

Thomas barely blocked it. It was as if the air had been stolen from his lungs. Mia had just been carried off before his eyes to her certain death at Wyvares. Whether wyvern truly existed and could be found there or not, Ilyron and Delia were ready to unleash their schemes on the Lowlands. Perhaps this was the end. The moment to accept he had failed in his duties and what lay ahead was beyond anything he could hope to slow, let alone stop.

Dodging to the side, Thomas deflected a strike from Ilsa's axe. An instant later, he managed to catch her whip strike with his forearm. Were he not wearing a rebrace inscribed with the burning words of the High King, he had no doubt it would have eviscerated his arm. As it was, he only felt the jarring impact and was forced back another step.

I can't just give up. I didn't give up when things were bleak on Emeral or outside Kirke or when we were captured at Kilkern's Redoubt. Anargen complimented me on my resilience in the face of adversity. It was one of the reasons Ecthelion chose to adopt me.

Once more, Ilsa launched an attack with her whip, and Thomas raised his sword-wielding forearm to catch it. Except this time, the whip wrapped around the arm, and she jerked him forward, her axe already swinging around to connect with his neck.

He levied a hasty block just managing to catch the axe with his shield and was thrown off balance. Ilsa didn't hesitate to deliver a hard kick straight to his abdomen that sent him tumbling onto the floor.

How did she uncoil her whip so fast?

The answer was obvious. Her whip was no more a common coil of leather than she was an innocent woman caught up in this. Ilsa was, in fact, a witch and wielded more power than her demure nature could ever have hinted at. Even now, as she looked on smiling, she seemed to tower over him like a giant. Had her arms grown thicker and her size increased that much? How was the room holding her? And her axe seemed to have become serrated and exuded a dark green energy.

And Thomas felt ... tired. So tired. Of running, of fighting, of watching everything he cared about fall apart. He leaned away from another snap of the whip, which now seemed to have a life of its own, twisting and coiling to strike like a live serpent. It, too, was sheathed in an eerie green aura.

"That's right, Thomas. You see, you have no hope. Don't make this harder on yourself than it has to be. What I'm offering you is quick. The Queen plans to use her powers to create a much more protracted end for the rest of her enemies."

Thomas's heart thudded in his chest as he realized very soon, he was going to die. Desperate, he swiped at the horrid monstrous version of Ilsa bearing down on him, her visage twisted into a dark mask that was her face but also terrifyingly other.

Her whip caught around the blade and she jerked back, seeking to wrench it from his hand.

No!

His grip held, but not for the strength of Thomas's fingers. It was as though the spiritsword itself refused to be parted from him. Refused to yield to someone who defied everything that formed its very substance.

"Foolish, little cur," Ilsa snarled. "Let it go. You're just a peasant. The son of a failure and yourself a miserable excuse for a guardian. You have no authority to defy me or the powers I wield."

Thomas tightened his grip on his spiritsword, a drowning man in a tempest-tossed sea clinging to the cork lifebuoy offered him. Heat from its flames warmed his skin, chasing away a chill he had scarcely noticed creeping up on him. The fire was irrepressible, coursing along the blade, undiminished, undeterred by Ilsa's swagger and threats. As much as he bore the spiritsword, Thomas understood at that moment, it was more than just an implement for his purposes. He was equally an implement. Thomas bore the High King's standard on his tunic. To the observer, it was either a humble if radiant lamb or a powerful and regal lion. But it was more than regalia or esoteric iconography. He was a lamb between the paws of the Great Lion.

Every feat he had accomplished, from the first until now, was beyond him. The steadfastness others prized in him was not his strength or resilience, but an imbuing like the fire crackling off his blade. His strength was bestowed on him by the Ruler of All Realms. And in Thomas's weakness, he knew that the High King's magnificent strength, which could shake the Lowlands into rubble at his choosing, would shine forth brightest.

That strength took hold of Thomas's limbs, his sinews, hardening his very bones with a resolve that he would never find in himself. Yanking back against Ilsa's pull, he felt her giving, skidding toward him.

Her eyes went wide, and for a moment, he saw through the façade. The mirage of a being of unparalleled power and prowess. She was no more so than other servants of the dark. A shadow that the High King's light could banish in an instant.

Thomas pulled once more, and as she staggered forward, he kicked off against her thighs and twisted the sword, so that as she tumbled backward, the burning blade cleaved through the dark coil wound around it.

Ilsa was back on her feet in an instant but gone was the illusion of her enormity. A husk of hatred and fear remained as she tossed aside the smoldering ruin of her whip. Thomas rose to his feet. The other remnant of her snake-like cord disintegrated off the spiritsword.

"We both know that no authority you possess, no powers you call upon, are anything compared to the High King of All Realms. While I'm a failure, and I'm a peasant, I'm also a Palatini Lucis Aeternae—Knight of Light—bound by oath to serve him, and as such, I represent him everywhere I go and before every foe I face.

"You have mastered artifice and deceit, but don't beguile yourself into believing the dark will overcome the light."

A hiss rose in Ilsa's throat, and she surged forward, using both hands to swing her axe overhead and bring down on his head. Thomas's shield was ready and bore blow after blow after blow.

Sending the last blow askew, Thomas pivoted, came around, and delivered a quick slice to the back of Ilsa's leg.

With a screech, she went down to one knee. Her free hand grabbed for her seared calf. She spat. "I suppose that was for how I poisoned that little pig's leg?"

Thomas felt sick. The attack had simply been a move meant to force Ilsa to yield. How had he been blind to the nature of the illness besetting Gregor? It was as if he'd kept his eyes closed for weeks. Maybe more. He had seen what Ilsa had wanted him to see. Had he not been too fixed on safeguarding everyone by his wit and will, he might have faced the truth of the darkness creeping around them in time to thwart her.

"Gregor will recover. The High King's fire doesn't just burn, it refines, removing dross and impurities to forge anew, to anneal."

Ilsa cocked her head to the side and ran her tongue over her still split lip. "And you think your fire will recast me, hmm? I'm far less broken than you, phosphila." Her lip jutted out in a pout, "Especially with what Queen Delia will do to your fate-spoken love?"

Clenching his jaw against a scathing retort, Thomas strained not to fall for her baiting. "You don't know the future any more than I do. Even if you worked to make sure I kept seeing only one end for us. Perhaps your time would be better served in reflecting on your own fate. Poisella so very nearly turned from the dark. You don't have to remain in it, you can escape it—even show her the way free from it."

"Fool!" Ilsa snarled. "I *am* the dark!" From within the fold of the cloak she wore, Ilsa flung a barrage of black knives.

Forced to block them with his shield, Thomas, sidestepped.

Ilsa's axe cleaved the air beside him and clattered off the stone. A chunk of the stone broke off from the force of the blow.

Seizing the moment as it unfolded, Thomas grazed Ilsa's back with his fiery sword.

Immediately her cloak caught fire in a way that suggested it was enchanted with dark sorceries. It took only a moment for the thing to be reduced to ashen tatters, and Thomas could only watch fixedly as Ilsa tried futilely to extinguish the flame.

Looking up at him with murderous rage contorting her face, Ilsa's flesh grew cloudy, discolored to an ashen hue. Ilsa drew a vile from a pouch at her waist and slammed it onto the stone floor. A haze of black smoke enveloped her.

She's going to turn to shadow and escape!

The fire on her cloak flared brighter, so much so Thomas had to shield his eyes. There was a shriek, whether of annihilation or escape, he couldn't be sure. When his eyes adjusted, there was no trace of Ilsa. As much as his baser nature feared that she was simply lurking in the shadows, working off still more her illusions, he was deeply convicted that she had lost her battle against the light.

Raising his helmet's faceplate, Thomas drew in a deep, shuddering breath and rubbed his face. This was only the foreshock of a far greater quake. Outside was an army seeking to destroy them all, and somewhere far beyond in this dreadful night, a beast that was once a woman who epitomized beauty to him carried the only woman he had ever loved to her doom.

Thomas's hand drifted to the spot where the parchment was tucked inside his armor. But he couldn't bring himself to open it, Not now. It didn't matter what it said. All that mattered was she was gone.

Instead, he walked over and picked up Sir Hurstwell's spiritsword. Mia had attempted to wield it, and he regretted not teaching her more. More about defense. But even so, far more about the High King of All Realms.

Looking down at the blade, he spotted the glowing lettering that he clung to with fierce need: "My grace is sufficient for you, for my power is made perfect in weakness."

Great King, thank you. You delivered me in this battle. Please, I need so much more of your strength for what lies ahead.

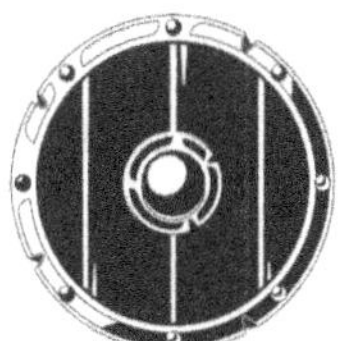

22

Dashing down the stairs, Thomas skidded to a halt in front of the infirmary. There, to his conflicting relief and dismay, were the Ecthel soldiers he'd sent to safeguard Gregor and Mia. They looked shaken up, but not injured, which begged the question—why were they still here?

Given what he'd just endured in Ilsa and Delia's escape, he was glad they had not shown up suddenly. Since they weren't able to safeguard Mia, they should, at the very least, be half a mile or more away from here and riding like the winds against the slopes of the Shield Islands for refuge at Caldoness.

By the time he was within five feet of the assembled soldiers, Sergeant Strathmore noticed his approach and walked over to intercept him. "Sir Fenwrest, my apologies. We were not able to leave to secure Baroness Sornfold. I trust you have succeeded where we have not?"

For once, Thomas's expression did not give away the truth, though he wished it had. It would have rescued him from having to taste the awful words in his mouth. "No. I did not.

The Baroness has been captured by ... Monarchist forces. I wasn't able to stop them before they took her."

Strathmore looked properly mortified by the news. Stroking his beard, he offered, "Perhaps they will attempt to ransom her. Trade her for Queen Delia."

Thomas closed his eyes to hold back the swell of shame and frustration that beset him. "They were able to escape with her as well. They had help from the Baroness's handmaiden. The Queen's capture was all part of a plan to get to the Viceroy and strike him down."

"By all in the Lowlands," the older man said, shaking his head in disbelief. "What an evil night this has been."

"It isn't over yet," Thomas reminded him, gruffer than he meant to. His eyes roved to the doorway the others were clustered around. "Is the Heir Apparent well?"

It was the Sergeant's turn to hedge at the question. "He lives, for now. It appears Steward Kilkern found the boy's infected leg to be beyond saving and amputated it shortly before the battle began. His bleeding hasn't fully stopped."

"What? That's not possible. He was walking just earlier," Thomas protested. "It wasn't good for him, but he was up and using his leg!"

Pursing his lip, the guard looked down to the stone floor. "I'm sorry to say, it's worse than that. Between the illness and blood loss, he is too weak to move and ... to be blunt, sir, I don't believe he will make it through the night."

Shaking his head, Thomas felt as though the room was literally tilting under him and braced himself on the wall. "No. No. No," he kept repeating as if just saying it was enough to undo the words he'd just heard. Ecthelion, Mia, Gregor— Ecthelowall's hopes were pinned on them. Was he really going to lose them all in one night?

Wringing his hands, Strathmore gave Thomas a minute to

steady himself before saying, "As his cousin, it would be proper for you to see him to the end."

Proper, but not practical. There was a battle happening outside, and every one of them was needed for it. But the pull of his heart to that quiet room was like the sea to the shore. Inevitably, he found himself standing inside its tight enclosure looking down on Gregor.

A thin sheen of sweat covered Gregor's brow, and he groaned. Gregor's eyes fluttered open and took several seconds before they seemed to focus enough on Thomas to recognize him. The boy coughed and hoarsely said, "Why are you loafing about here? Shouldn't you be defending the castle?"

It was a needed glimmer of spring warmth amidst cold hard truths he was facing. An ensuing coughing fit and the shivers that wracked Gregor's too-small body drug Thomas back into somberness. Worst was his inability to look away from the flattened area beneath the blanket where the lower portion of Gregor's left leg should have been.

"The defense can spare me. I had to check on you."

"Come to say goodbye, hmm?"

Thomas gaped. The room and Gregor's demeanor had grown icy in an instant. "No, no ..." His attempt to protest fell flat. He could think of nothing else to say.

Gregor snorted and looked away from him. "I heard what they said in the hall. I'm dying." He was seized by a coughing fit and moaned as if to confirm it. "I suppose it's just as well that I go now. It sounds like things have gone to bits on you."

"They could be better," Thomas admitted, feeling as if the specter of it all was there, crushing his heart in its inescapable grasp. Hearing Gregor talk like this, his tone that of the old Gregor, full of disdain and self-centeredness, only tightened that vice-like grip.

"I'm sorry for you and Mia. I suppose we were all fate-spoken and didn't even know it."

Fate-spoken, as though from the beginning they were doomed to this path. Unable to have any hope, any future but this tragic one. "No," Thomas objected, taking a seat beside Gregor's bed and resting heavily on the hilt and cross guard of Sir Hurstwell's spiritsword. "I don't believe that for a second."

Gregor eyed him with a rich mixture of fear and desperation and hopefulness, but it all muddied into resignation, despair. "I thought that too. Till I came in here to rest and Kilkern checked my leg. Told me I had the Devastation in it and my exertion had burst the pustules of infection, releasing it into the rest of my body. You know he told me it was pointless to do so, but he was going amputate my leg to ease things for me. As if it could!"

Thomas's eyes jerked from where they held to the floor to Gregor's leg. Steward Kilkern the Physician might not have been caring for his cousin at all. That Kilkern, the real Kilkern, was likely already dead and forsaken. So, all of this, the treatments, amputation, even the infection with the Devastation, were by the hands of Ilsa and the thing the Viceroy called a doppelganger. Both of them deceptive creatures of darkness intending to destroy Gregor.

Where his face and hands touched the sword, Thomas felt a flush of heat. The blade was reacting to the dark sorceries at work. "Dark must flee the light," he muttered to himself, mulling what to do. If this was indeed all the work of that monster, then surely the High King's fire could undo it. The glimpse of such wonder gripped Thomas, forcing the icy hands of despair to loose their hold on his heart.

How my King? How can he be delivered from this?

"Thomas," Gregor spoke up, his voice a low, tremulous

whisper. "Why is this happening to me? Why is the High King, if he's out there, letting evil win?"

He leaned forward, earnest. "The High King isn't letting evil win."

"Then he can't stop what's happening to us," Gregor accused, another coughing fit seizing him.

Thomas waited for the fit to subside. He rested his chin back on the spiritsword as he watched his young cousin struggling to hold onto life. There was no denying the High King had the power to end all of this. But it felt so difficult to convey. Gregor hadn't had the vision, hadn't seen the High King and felt the overwhelming magnificence of his light.

"You can't answer," Gregor wheezed. "Because there isn't one. That's why when you got hurt rescuing me on the cliff face, you couldn't say why the High King let it happen. And why Sirt Hurstwell was killed in battle. And why I'm dying now ..."

"No!" Thomas clanked the tip of Hurstwell's spiritsword into the stone floor. "I just ... I'm not the wisest Knight. I've only been in the High King's service about two years, and I'm just now forming the words to express it for myself."

Nodding at the sword, Gregor quipped, "Shouldn't the answer be etched there? Even now, I see the inscriptions glowing faintly."

Thomas regarded the spiritsword, the fire imbued in it was hardly dying embers.

No, that's just Gregor. He's drifting away.

"I'm sure it is on here. I study and I train with the sword when I can, but I haven't yet been shown that. Things are revealed in the High King's timing and wisdom."

"Humph, what is wise about us dying? Our country being ruined? Mia being taken?"

Thomas drew in a sharp breath and jammed the sword down again, hard enough to chip the stone. "I wish I could explain it to you. When you pledge yourself to be his no matter what happens, he pledges that you are his no matter what happens. Good and bad in the Lowlands continue, but the King's Day will come, and everything will be new."

"That feels like an easy answer," Gregor countered, trying to push himself up on his elbows and dropping back down with a groan of effort. "I need something, anything, tangible."

He gave a shrug. "Hard questions sometimes are that not because the answer is difficult to find, but because accepting it can be. Sometimes, we make obscure what should be clear."

"Forgive me for not swallowing that with ease. Maybe things would be clearer if my eyes weren't darkened by the Devastation and all I'm suffering! I thought you would understand after all you've lost."

That was a good point. Thomas had been through a lot in his relatively short life. He had once thought his early days were fraught because of losing his parents and birthright. It could scarcely compare to what he had gone through to get Mia and Gregor safely off Emeral and the Isle of Geists. Even that seemed now only a pale shadow of the hardships to be endured. Mere practice for this, the actual test.

Thomas gasped. He couldn't help it. It felt as if his heart had just thrust open the doors of his mind in an invasion and demanded his mind submit to a truth it had been unwilling to see until now.

"Everything in our lives has been shaping us to face this moment, Gregor. Can you see that? Each hardship, each pain forged us to stand before the storm battering us now. Maybe even this, even the tumult we face, is only to prepare us for something yet to come. Something we could never weather without having passed through these harrowing straits."

Brows furrowed, Gregor regarded Thomas for a moment before closed his eyes and gritted his teeth against a sharp swell of pain. Through his teeth, he countered, "Maybe you can see it that way. But why should we suffer? Why can't the High King just lift us out of it instead? Do I look like I'll be ready to face anything but the grave?"

"What is our allegiance worth if we only grant it when things are good and easy?" Thomas rebuffed with a gentleness. "You keep telling me what we're losing. Consider what we gain in the end. A better kingdom. The men of the Lowlands for millennia have been in rebellion against their Rightful King. Even those who knew him and saw him. Perhaps we are proven true in our steadfastness."

"Even to death?" Gregor asked hoarsely. "My death? Mia's death? Your death, which can't be far off now?"

"Yes." Thomas pinned his younger cousin with his most earnest stare. "I know the One to whom I've committed myself. He deserves all I have to give. Every bead of sweat, every fallen tear, and every drop of blood. Whether I am rewarded or not. He deserves my allegiance."

The boy turned his head, staring at the wall. After a few moments, he said in worrisomely quiet, mewling voice, "I'm scared, Thomas. I wish I could be brave like you. I thought I could ... could be like you and Sir Hurstwell. I'm not. All I can do is lie here, terrified of death as it swallows me whole."

His head whipped around and there was a wildness in his eyes. "Don't leave! Don't let the shadows take me here, alone, so far from home."

Thomas put his hand on his cousin's arm, firm as he dared. It felt so thin, so fragile to his touch. "I won't leave you alone," he soothed.

Sounds of rapid footsteps and shouting filled the hallway outside the room. Beyond the doorway Strathmore called out, moving to intercept whomever was charging through the corridor and almost immediately reversed course and backed deeper into the hallway, allowing a small group of soldiers and other men to careen into the room.

23

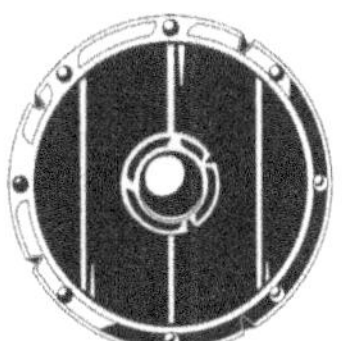

A quartet of Ecthel soldiers bore a bier into the confines of the infirmary. They dropped the patient laying atop the bedding across from Thomas and Gregor and then scattered, making room for some castle physicians to rush in and apply their craft. Before they could block his line of sight, Thomas saw who they'd brought in.

He covered his mouth with his palm, hoping to mask the anxiousness he knew he couldn't hide from his face. It was the Viceroy. He looked even worse than when Thomas had left him. Pale, so very pale, and breathing shallowly. Ecthelion was going to die, just like Sir Hurstwell had, and there was nothing Thomas could do to prevent it.

"I should return to the battle," he said softly, gripping the arms of the chair he sat in. Knowing he had just promised not to leave Gregor, but Gregor wasn't alone now, and ... how was Thomas supposed to stay and watch them both die? It would rend him apart!

"What's that?" One of the soldiers who brought Ecthelion in asked as he passed by, heading for the hallway.

Straightening and forcing himself to keep a rein on his emotions, Thomas replied, "I need to get back out to the battle. Lend my support."

"What support could you add?" the man groused. He stopped, cocked his head to the side, regarding Thomas as if he was crazy and then his eyes widened in recognition. "Sir Fenwrest ... er ... Halifax, my humble apologies."

Waving it off, Thomas replied, "You may be right. The situation was dire when I came to secure the Baroness and Heir Apparent." He couldn't bring himself to say he had failed on both counts.

The soldier was one of Ecthelion's personal guards, Andrew Lancaster, Thomas recalled. He smoothed back his tangle of sandy locks and shook his head. Strong-jawed, solidly built, he was only about a decade older than Thomas, but his face, caked with silt from the fens, seemed a century old. "Begging your pardon, sir. You have missed much. The battle is over."

Looking around at everyone in the room, Thomas protested, "How can that be? The castle hasn't fallen."

Lancaster let a wan smile slip onto his face and he stroked the stubble of a beard he had grown. "If there is anything good to be said for this day, it is that the most unexpected things happened to both sides of the war."

Thomas crossed his arms over his chest. "What do you mean, Lancaster?"

The soldier swallowed, seeming to chafe under being identified. "I, um, well, we were being overrun by the Emeralans and those, uh, those creatures. The carrion they're called, as I understand."

Thomas grimaced. "I would not call them creatures. They are men and women whose minds are under the control of a spell."

"Beg your pardon again, sir. Those are awfully violent and stalwart people. They advanced with no regard for their own safety. No hesitancy when injured mortally. Just battering and tearing at everyone they encounter without mercy."

"That is the nature of the spell." Thomas remembered his brush with death at the hands of similar brutes.

"Yes, well, we were almost overwhelmed by them when some kind of enormous dark carrion fowl flew from the castle and soared off into the night. We thought for sure it was a bad omen and meant we were doomed.

"But by whatever powers—maybe your king's—must have decreed fates be reversed, because not ten minutes later, all the carrion began dropping. All of them, either dead or unconscious."

Standing, Thomas grabbed the messenger by the arms. "You're jesting. They just fell?"

"I saw it with my own eyes. By the hundreds. They just sank to the ground, still as the grave. It startled all of us, but the Emeralans were thrown into a panic. They had the numbers to win the day even without the carrion, but they were so unnerved by it, they fled. This time when we pursued, we overtook them. Many escaped, but they won't dare try an advance like this again."

Sinking back into his chair, Thomas stared up at the stones of the ceiling unable to speak. Either Delia or Ilsa must have been the one to cast the carrion spell on those within their army. Whether by destruction or distance of the spellcaster, it appeared the hold was broken. Which raised the question, if any of them lived, what would be left of the person who had been so possessed?

"I don't blame the Emeralans for running," Lancaster added, almost offhanded. "It looks as though every last one of those carrion soldiers was the dead walking."

Thomas arched a brow, pulled sharply from his pondering by that sentiment.

Lancaster clarified, "They all had the Devastation. Worse than even him," he said, pointing to Gregor. "Pale as snow with palms and eyes black as if they'd been painted in pitch. Creepiest thing I've seen in all my days."

Rubbing the back of his neck, Thomas didn't bother commenting. Something about this all was significant. But what? What did it mean that those who should have been lying immobilized in pain, drawing each numbered breath with great effort, could run and leap and bite and fight?

"Pity we never found the cause of the Devastation. That Kilkern seemed as if he was our best chance at managing it. Seemed to know more about it than anyone."

After a minute of silence, Lancaster cleared his throat. "With your leave, sir, I am needed outside. There are plenty of injured, and the sooner we get them away from the rotting corpses riddled with the Devastation, the better chance they have of surviving."

"Of course." Thomas stood and gave him a salute. "Hale evening, ever before the dawn of Ecthelowall's Commonwealth."

Lancaster nodded and dashed out, already several minutes behind the others of his company.

Watching Lancaster leave the room and then the two physicians attending Ecthelion for a minute, Thomas felt lightheaded. He dropped back into his seat and shot a glance at his cousin. The boy, miserable as he was, looked wonderstruck. This was such a turn from before they had been intruded upon by the others.

As he stared at Gregor's Devastation-ravaged face, the tumblers of his thoughts clicked into place.

That's it. That's what is going on. Impossible as it sounds, it must be the answer.

Rising abruptly, he reached to take Gregor's spiritsword. He found the boy's grip surprisingly resilient. "Trust me," Thomas instructed. "You want to be free from the shadows, right? To escape the dark?"

"Yes," Gregor wheezed his gaze settling from startled into purely desperate.

"Then I know how to help."

Gregor frowned, his blackened eyes, like all of him, seeming so exhausted that they couldn't be far from their last sleep. Gradually, he relinquished his hold on it.

Thomas lifted it slowly away, having become acutely aware that the physicians in the room had paused from tending to Ecthelion, each looking ready to leap on him if the need called for it.

Drawing in a breath to steady himself, Thomas looked toward the south and east, where he knew the Highlands looked down on them all. He uttered a silent plea and as flames raced up the spiritsword, he pulled back the blanket over Gregor's amputated leg.

Almost gagging at the stench of putrification, he angled the sword and brought the flat of it against Gregor's ravaged flesh. The burning letters flared brighter, a chorus of whispered words danced with the flames from the blade onto the boy's leg, racing up it, setting it aglow. An instant later, the flames had traced to his eyes, his palms, crisscrossing his entire small body.

"*Ah!*" Gregor cried out, seizing as the fire did its work.

"What have you done?" cried out one of the physicians.

"Guards!" yelled the other, who took up a defensive position.

In rushed Sergeant Strathmore with his supporting

subordinates. Sword drawn, his eyes jumped from the physician to Thomas and back again. "What is wrong?"

"Bind him!" the physician who called for them instructed, pointing to Thomas. He struck our patient with his sword. The pain it caused him alone could kill him. Not to mention the danger of letting the Devastation's odors and humors spread to all of us!"

Strathmore regarded Thomas carefully, weighing whether the fiery display he was witnessing was, in fact, good or the horrific attack it appeared. All of it, doubtless was hinging on how much he trusted Thomas after the earlier displays he'd witnessed.

For a full minute, his eyes held steady on Thomas before fixing on the blade, still pressed to Gregor's leg. He squinted and then took a step back. "That's your spiritsword, isn't it?"

"Sir Hurstwell left this one to Gregor, actually," Thomas replied.

"The fire on it, it's coursing along his body. Is it hurting him?" Strathmore asked, pointing to where the flames were starting to burn lower, but still emitted warmth and an amber glow.

The first physician peered around Thomas, clearly shocked to be hearing about fire when there was no smoke. His eyes widened, and he looked back at his colleague.

"I can't say whether it's painful or not, only that it's all I can do to save his life," Thomas answered. "What Lancaster told me of the battle outside. The carrion. I think the Devastation isn't a common illness. It's—"

"Of course, it's not a *common illness*," chided the physician who still protected Ecthelion with his body. "It's sent thousands to their beds, forced families apart as their loved ones were sent to die in Kilkern's Redoubt."

The way the man said it made Thomas wonder who he had lost to the Devastation. "And that's the key," Thomas picked up. "They were sent to Kilkern's Redoubt. By the hundreds. Only ..." Thomas hedged at introducing such strange and terrible truths.

"It was part of Ilyron's stratagem. A ruse," Ecthelion spoke up, his voice terribly weak and yet authoritative. "Please, do not interrupt my heir again," he commanded, pushing up onto his elbows.

The physician looked as if he would never be able to close his mouth again. Fortunately, Strathmore wasn't so thrown and picked up the conversation. "What does the Monarch want with the victims of the Devastation? And why stow them at Kilkern's Redoubt?"

Thomas gestured toward outside the room and the castle. "Lancaster said those carrion were afflicted with the Devastation. They should be immobilized, but instead sounded just as ferocious, if not more so. I know from stories ..." Thomas had to catch himself, "From histories, I mean, that the carrion's curse works best on those with the resistance to it diminished. I think the Monarch used his dark sorcery to make the Devastation what it is and to raise an army. One we would never see coming, never guard against, and never be able to stop by conventional means."

When Thomas paused and gave a look of prompting, Strathmore scratched his chin in thought but looked as if he was drawing a blank. Maybe this wasn't all as obvious and certain as Thomas had concluded.

"The sick of Kilkern's Redoubt. He's going to use them to capture the northlands," Ecthelion concluded and dropped back to his bed with a gasp. "They'll be turned into carrion and used to destroy everyone in their path."

Ecthelion's closest physician shushed and said, "Your

Honor, please rest. A fever is making you speak wildly. I'll send this mad boy away."

Grumbling, Ecthelion pushed the man away. "I do not need your skepticism for my cure. I am a Knight of Light and have seen far more startling things." He drew in a deep breath, seeming to shore himself up. "And I will not be made to repeat myself again. The *mad boy* is my adoptive son and heir. You will accord him all due honors and respect."

With that, the tension in Ecthelion's frame went slack and he breathed in shallowly. The exertion had taken too much from him. From the stress wrinkling the physician's brow, it had taxed him as well. Crestfallen, he started to mumble something multiple times without completing a single sentence.

While the healer dithered over how to respond, Thomas concluded, "The Viceroy is right. Monarch Ilyron will use the carrion, and I think I know where they will march first —Wyvares."

"No," a new voice added to the discourse.

Thomas's heart hammered in his chest, the thrill of hope realized threatening to burst him from within. "Gregor!"

His younger cousin's complexion was much rosier, haler than he'd seen him in more than a week. From the way he lay, it was clear Gregor wasn't going to be jumping out of the bed, but the flames had faded, and there was spark in his gaze that Thomas had never seen there before. In fact, there was far more to him now, and Thomas could hardly contain his awe.

He had the vision.

Gregor shot Thomas a wry smile. "You were right," he said. "Once you've seen him, it changes how you see everything. Yielding to him shifts all of this into focus." Clearing his throat, which sounded more choked with emotion than constricted by weakness and disease, he added, "He showed me what is coming next."

24

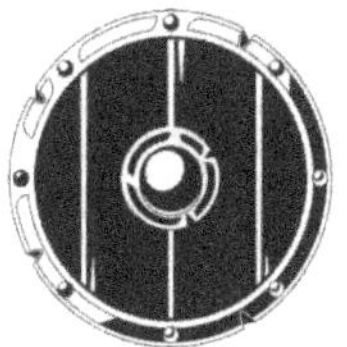

Night's hold over the jagged landscape was absolute, lacking even a single star to break up the bleakness. By the light shining from his armor, Thomas could see little gleams of white. Twisting and drifting, the tiny flakes of the persistent snows had beset them ever since they crossed deep into the Upper Albar Mountains. Ahead, he could make out their guide raising his arm to signal they should halt.

Thomas relayed the message with a wave to those following him. It was hard to say, but he thought Sergeant Strathmore understood. There were only two dozen of them in total, all that Viceroy Ecthelion was willing to send on the task of recovering Mia.

Had anyone other than Ecthelion insisted on such a small band for sneaking into Queen Delia's camp to rescue Mia and slip back through the mountains, Thomas would've argued vehemently. But Ecthelion barely clung to life, and Gregor, or *Sir* Gregor as Thomas should get used to calling him, had insisted the High King showed him the same path. After receiving a fiery treatment similar to Gregor's, Steward

177

Malcolm was recovering. In thanks, he provided two guides for this journey. Albarons who knew these mountains better than their own names.

Those names were Ulster and Fenwick, at least Thomas thought that was what they'd told him. He wasn't sure. Twins, they were chosen for having grown up among these elevations. It certainly showed. The dark-haired men were like the mountains. Rugged, solid, and cold. Few words passed from them, and like the sporadic howling winds rushing through the peaks, they were quick, loud, and abrasive. One twin was at the front of the column, one at the back. Trusting them in their reticence would have been impossible if they didn't seem to know where every loose stone along the treacherous paths were and the location of every patch of wild berries in the glens safe to eat.

"Sir, not to belabor the point," Strathmore began, breaking from the planned single file column approach they had been given to come alongside Thomas, "but the men are getting restless. Are we nearing Wyvares or not? Frederick swore he saw tents and lights in a vale below. There's concern we're walking in circles. Or worse, into a trap."

Thomas clenched his jaw to keep from letting loose a sigh. Even someone of Strathmore's years couldn't hold patient much longer. "I don't know," he admitted with a shrug.

"Good thing, we do," a husky voice replied from a few steps ahead of Thomas. Ulster, Thomas guessed, had his arms crossed over his broad chest. He nodded over his shoulder. "We're there. We brought you around from the northern face of the mountain pass. The Monarchists won't anticipate that."

Thomas scrambled up to where Ulster stood, kicking up fine powdery snow as he did. He popped a couple dubh berries harvested from brambles on the lower slopes. The dark berries' sweetness, cut with a tart edge, filled his mouth. He hoped they would give him energy and an edge for what lay ahead.

From his vantage he could see the camp clearly. Frederick had been right about glimpsing it before. There could only be about fifteen or so soldiers encamped there, far fewer than Thomas expected. Many fewer than the thousands the Monarchists could now send, given they had turned the Devastation into a malevolent tool of control. When Gregor told him the High King wanted them to take this path, it hadn't made sense. Something added was going on, something they hadn't quite sorted out yet. There wasn't time to do so. Gregor had also confirmed the fears that Steward Kilkern had hinted to them about Wyvares. Yes, there was a wyvern to awake here, but it was so much worse than that. The Monarchists were going to use forbidden Tislatnean spells to create a dragon. Something so hideously evil, the entire realm of Tislatna had been destroyed millennia ago to expunge it.

With Ulster and his brother's unapproved roundabout approach, they might be too late. Even now, one of the scaly menaces could be watching them with immeasurable coolness and cruelty.

What sort of signs needed they look for? Wyverns and dragons weren't exactly a subject matter well-covered in the texts he'd been required to read as a page and squire to Hurstwell. Anargen had said precious little about the wyvern he faced in Stormridge, other than it was the most menacing beast he'd yet witnessed.

"Strathmore," Thomas waved the other man over. "Look, I want you to take half the men and come down straight at the camp along this route." To Ulster, Thomas turned and said, "You and Fenwick take the rest farther down and attack from the western flank."

"Not to quibble with you over your orders, sir," Strathmore

said, clearing his throat and keeping his eyes down on the camp. "But couldn't we all attack together and overrun them? They look to barely have half our number."

"They've been one step ahead of us this whole time," Thomas reminded him. "Their Queen engages in dark sorceries, and, if I understand the legends rightly, in order to summon a dragon, she will need a goblin to bind to the wyvern. You saw the werebeasts that attacked Dirkforge, what havoc and horror they inflicted. They would seem sweet dreams compared to the nightmare of even one dark elf."

Strathmore's eyes widened, and he swallowed uncomfortably. "Very well, sir. I can see why the Viceroy put you in our command."

"A two-prong attack is a bold risk to take upon us," Ulster pointed out as he tested the sharpness of his battle axe. "It will require impressive timing with my band taking the extra circuitous route."

He's surprisingly well-spoken when he chooses to speak up. I wonder if Fenwick is as well.

"It is, and I would not ask you to bear the greatest risk. I'm going to go down first. I will give you the sign to attack when the moment is right."

Placing his hand on Thomas's shoulder, Strathmore said, "Sir, forgive me, but battling an entire camp alone? That is too dangerous for any of us, especially you. Remember, you're not a simple squire or even just a Knight of Light now. You're the future Baron of Halifax. It would be best to keep you safely on the ridge while we battle."

Thomas gripped Strathmore's shoulder in kind. "The Baroness is down there, Sergeant. I can't risk the Queen harming her if she feels cornered. I'm going to get the Baroness first, and then I'll gladly have you rush to my aid."

He could see the other wasn't totally convinced. Even

Ulster had arched a brow at him. Gnawing on his lip, debating about it, he decided there was no point in dancing around the truth at this crucial juncture. Certainly not with either of these men. "Besides, if I don't do all I can to rescue the Baroness and something happens to her, I'm not sure there will be much left of me to yet lose."

Strathmore rubbed his face as if that was the worst news he could get. "Lowlands be scoured and you wouldn't find such ill fortune. You two are fate-spoken!"

Shirking Strathmore's hold on him, Thomas leveled a hard stare at the man. "The High King of All Realms alone knows our ends. If he deems I fall this night, you could scour the Lowlands for every warrior, bard, and prophet to speak to the contrary, and it would still come to pass. But, if he bids me stand, then not even a dragon will be able to thwart me, or us."

Twiddling his thumbs a bit, Strathmore wouldn't totally concede but did at length give a resigned nod. Needing nothing more than his compliance, Thomas addressed Ulster. "Ready the men you find best suited to navigating to the position I gave you. Watch for the sign and give them all you have when you see it."

Ulster nodded. "Very well. If I may inquire, what form or nature will the sign take?"

"You'll know it when you see it," Thomas replied as he got into position. "May the High King's favor be upon you." He began sliding surreptitiously down the slope.

May the High King guide me to that sign and Mia to rescue.

25

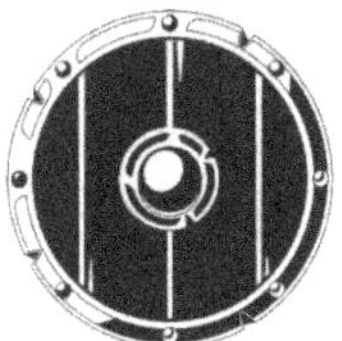

The Monarchist camp was preternaturally quiet. Thomas spotted a fire burning in the center of the camp. A few soldiers stood around it, seeming oddly at ease for such a nefarious purpose as the one they pursued. Could Delia have deceived these men about her aims here? Or worse, were they darkling creatures themselves and so at ease with evil, they luxuriated in it as a man would the warm sun in a frigid place like this?

Slinking along the periphery of the camp, he kept an eye on the soldiers by the fire. Even though he felt sure every crunch of his feet on the snow would alert them to his presence, the Monarchists didn't betray any signs of even being casually aware of their surroundings. They were still as stone, more statues than men.

Why it bothered him so much was hard to put into words. There was no way to say from this distance that the men were anything but disciplined. Whatever the case, their fixedness made his task easier. For the moment.

He came up to the first tent he could peer into, knowing that without any sounds to guide him, he had just as much chance of finding Monarchists as Mia waiting within.

Taking in a deep breath, he threw open the flap and ducked inside, his spiritsword drawn.

"Oof!"

He fell backward and hit the ground. Standing inches from where he just came in was one of them. A Monarchist soldier, garbed in green, standing stock still, his eyes fixed to the distance. Specifically, the south. So much so that his back was mostly to Thomas.

In spite of the noise, the soldier didn't turn to face Thomas. Didn't even deflect his dazed stare one inch.

Thomas regarded the man for several seconds. He was pale, and his features gaunt. Under his eyes was the dark bruising of the Devastation. Thomas realized this individual was an Emeralan, rather than an Ecthel or Albaron. That meant Delia had sent him here in advance of the attack on Dirkforge. Sheathing his spiritsword with great caution, he regarded the man in the low light of a centrally burning candle. Thomas noticed there was a faint, foreign smell in the air—incense. Not the sweet-smelling stuff Delia had used on him. This smelled like rotten eggs and molded stone. Circling the man, his hairs standing on end, Thomas observed that the man's lips were actually moving in a faint continuous chant of sorts.

He had no fixed reason why yet, but Thomas felt dread overtake him. Something very bad was happening.

Thomas slipped back out amd made straight for the largest tent in the camp. Pushing aside both flaps, he stormed in, drawing his spiritsword, expecting to find Delia standing there reciting some kind of incantation. Except it, too, was empty apart from Delia's litter and a haze of the foul odored incense.

Where is she?

He rummaged through the belongings finding a few scrolls with text written in a language he couldn't read but that looked very old. Outside there was a low rumbling sound that built to what could only be termed a roar.

Thomas dashed out again and looked toward a southern peak. There was now a dark maroon glow issuing midway up its height. From this angle, he could make out strange delineations in the slope at semi regular intervals.

Stairs?

Snow hadn't yet covered them, so they must have been cleared recently. Again, the sound echoed in the valley from the peak. This time louder, more forceful, as if the first were tentative, probing, and this an assertion. A declaration of doom.

Climbing up the crude steps, Thomas found a landing at their top with an opening into the mountain. It wasn't clear if it was a natural cave, an entry to some kind of temple, or both. Half collapsed and iced over columns were evocative of bared fangs, glistening with the hunger of the frigid beast. As if stepping past this point was to be devoured.

Stop it. There is nothing in the Lowlands for a servant of the High King to fear.

Following a rough stoney path deeper in, Thomas wished he had the others with him. He was standing on the edges of a giant open chamber, unambiguous now in its adoration of its idol. Tall stone pillars with red and black banding filled the room. On each were blockish depictions of men and women mixed with dragons and square designs.

Tislatnean pictographs.

Every noble born Ecthel had seen at least one supposed relic of the Lost Realm, and on these, the wyvern or dragon was shown great deference. The blocky pillars ringed the room in a horseshoe shape of increasing height as they reached the center of the cavern. Between the two tallest pillars was a recess.

As Thomas's eyes traced down from that point, he noticed the cut stone flooring glistened in little glassy ripples out from there as if an enormous wave had washed out from the recess and flash frozen from the cold. An awful feeling that something had once been imprisoned in ice and now was being unleashed from its frosty prison gripped him.

In the room's center was another focal point—a raised, expansive dais. On it stood Delia, her arms churning and swirling as she performed some sort of ritual dance. Smokes of various incenses wafted from censors hung around her. The dark tendrils almost seemed alive with the way they twisted, turned, and bunched like flying serpents encircling Delia and the dozen or so soldiers with her, who chanted something in a low monotone that sounded hollow even as it filled the chamber.

Dominating the space, however, was the source of the roars. Shaking its head, its scales slick with newly melted ice and snow, was a wyvern.

Whatever Thomas had imagined from the few tales he'd heard of wyvern, this beast exceeded them for terror. It was beyond enormous. Sleek scales in a deep green shade that evoked dread of poisons and every danger from the deepest wilds. On its snout was a frontal horn thrusting upward, jagged and prominent over its long face. It was a bit like the crocodiles that lived in the rivers of Anstara. A crest bridged two additional boney horn-like protrusions rising from its head like a terrible crown. Hundreds of pointed serrated teeth ringed its jaws, and a serpentine tongue flicked out at intervals as if tasting the air for the fear it seemed all too aware it would induce. Little sulfurous gusts issued from its maw as it huffed for reasons Thomas could only guess.

Timed to the loudest and most fervent incantations, the wyvern flexed powerful arms banded with muscles that held aloft its enormous leathery wings. Each wing bore one wicked, hooked talon that looked like it could gore a man. Though they were nothing next to the bony barbs running along its spine and adorning its tail.

Unnerving ochre eyes flicked back and forth with the keenness of not just a predator but one that seemed to comprehend everything about its far weaker prey. Most unsettling was the knowledge that this imposing and brutal beast was currently only that, a beast. Merely the vessel for something far more terrible. If the stories were true, and a goblin's possession of it produced a sapient and malevolent dragon, then Thomas shuddered to imagine the horrors it would unleash on the Lowlands.

Thomas had to keep himself steady. His heartbeat thundered in his ears, fighting the rhythm of the chant, implicitly rejecting it as profane without even knowing the words. Nothing about this was okay. His spiritsword burned hotter, furious over the wicked display taking place.

The chanting grew louder and louder. Clearly discernible, all the more with the echoes reverberating off the walls, the words were no less an enigma to him.

All of it fell away when Thomas saw her. Mia, chained at the wrists and ankles, was towed onto the central dais by a pair of soldiers. They didn't even break their chant. It was impossible to tell how Mia was from here, but Thomas knew if he didn't move fast, what happened next would be unambiguously heartbreaking.

Rising from where he had crouched behind an icy pillar, Thomas readied himself for the sprint over to her. But he couldn't take a step. Not even one.

Could the spell Delia was casting be barring him, blocking him from advancing to attack?

My King, help me!

A rush of heat enveloped him, and Thomas realized it wasn't Delia holding him back—it was the High King. He forbade Thomas to move forward.

No, no, please, my King! Don't let Mia be murdered. Especially not for that abomination!

The same pressure holding him back began lifting his arm until his hand rested on the pommel of Hurstwell's spiritsword. Thinking he understood, Thomas drew it. Acting on what he perceived to be the High King's directing, he raised the sword into the air. Fire raced up the blade in a brilliant blaze. Thomas saw it caught Mia's attention just as she reached the central dais. She seemed to notice him and went rigid.

All of the chanting stopped, and Delia's dance ended. She shouted something in the language Thomas didn't understand and drew a long dagger that curved a bit at the end like a snake in mid slither.

Presenting it before the wyvern, she said something else in the vicious-sounding foreign tongue and circled Mia like a predator its prey. Spitting words at her with an almost angry glee.

Behind her, the wyvern tensed, scraping its claws eagerly into the stone. It reminded Thomas of a cat preparing to receive a treat. His chest felt like the stone under the wyvern, crushed, eviscerated. Even so, he couldn't lower his raised sword if he wanted to. He glanced up at it, desperate to move.

A series of inscriptions flared brighter: "The High King will fight for you, only be silent."

Thomas tightened his grip on the spiritsword's hilt and strained to lift it higher. A tear slid down his cheek as he watched Mia, unmoving, still staring in his direction.

The chanting resumed and reached a feverish intensity, with the largely still observers now entering the same wild dance Delia had performed, if more stiffly. At the epicenter of the madness, Delia cried out again and stopped with her back to the wyvern. With a quick thrust, she plunged the dagger into Mia's abdomen.

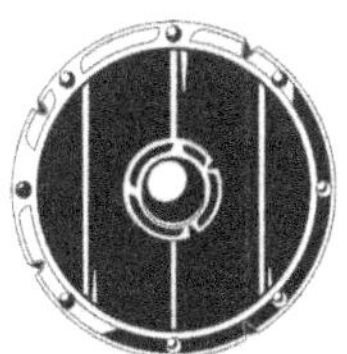

A dazzling flash of light filled the chamber that could not be masked or deflected or resisted. In spite of its brilliance, Thomas found his eyes could still focus. He blinked all the same. In between Mia and Delia was a blade. This one burning and wielded by a tall figure with armor that shimmered in the light as if it wasn't just ablaze but was formed from fire. The man-like figure stepped back the same instant Delia recoiled with a screech. The dagger in her hand, which looked black as night in the light, was disintegrating.

As if oblivious to Delia's screams and writhing as black smoke rolled off her hand holding the dagger, the stranger sheathed his sword and faced Mia. She had been very still through all of it, but suddenly jerked, as if coming out of a trance.

Or a vision ... Had she had the vision?

There was no time to answer the question. The stranger scooped her up in his arms and raced forward, through the throngs of blinded and staggering Monarchists, making straight for Thomas. He reached him in what seemed an instant later and placed Mia back on the ground. She, like Thomas, looked breathless over what had just transpired.

"Palatini Lucis Aeternae, do not gawk. You must get out of this chamber and ready yourself. The beast will only be stunned and will soon seek vengeance for what it was just denied."

Even the man's voice echoed with an intensity as of fire. Nothing close to the High King's as Thomas remembered, but still more than just a man.

Taller than Thomas and wearing armor made of interlocking plates of a silvery polished metal, he wore a helmet that sheathed his head like a hood and went down over his back. The opening in the helmet around his face revealed a visage like molten bronze and eyes with the fury to incinerate a man. As Thomas stared on, he couldn't help bumbling—amid the chaos and danger and wonder—"Who are you?"

At first, a quirk of the stranger's eyebrow was all his reaction to the question. When Thomas continued to gape, he spoke in quick clipped sentences. "My name is beyond your speech. I am a servant as you of the High King of All Realms. The Great King sent me. This is not the day for such evil to be permitted."

"Not the day for such evil," Thomas parroted. "Who ... what ..."

The stranger blinked. "If you must have a name for me, it can be Vif. Now, steel yourself. You and your beloved sister must face the beast and the witch."

Thomas blinked, looking to Mia, whose eyes were wide as well. "Where are you going?" he asked, unwilling to let this Vif depart. If they had to face a wyvern and Delia's wrath, surely they would need him.

"I must face the one the witch summoned. Go."

With that, he whirled around and zipped back toward the

central dais. The light around them faded back to normal levels. Thomas's eyes still did not need to adjust. He felt as if he'd been plunged into the sea depths by a tempest and, in a blink of the eye, was dry as if he'd walked through a desert. Had he really just seen ... just spoken to ... an elf?

"I, um, wait ..." Thomas stared across the room, unsure what to think or feel or do. The soldiers who had been only half present were now more animated, rubbing their eyes and groaning as if they had been clubbed. Delia clutched her singed hand, which seemed so much like the staged injury from Ilsa, it was eerie. Behind all of them, the wyvern thrashed and stumbled, its talons digging grooves into the stone floor. It shook its enormous head and bellowed out angry roars between hissed whimpers.

Mia turned his head toward her and lifted the face plate. Looking him in the eyes, she called over the cacophony, "You came for me."

"Of course," he replied, still breathy with wonderment over what was happening around them.

"We have to get out of here. We must trust Vif."

There was such earnest in her eyes, it gave Thomas pause. He stroked her cheek with his thumb and kissed her on the forehead. A storm tide of emotions hammered him, and he choked out, "Okay."

Outside the chamber, the wind had kicked up. It howled through the mouth of the cavern with as much ferocity as the wyvern within. They ran, stumbling down the stairs and deep into the camp before stopping to stand at the entrance of an empty Monarchist tent. Snow flew in at a slant, making it difficult to see more than a few steps ahead. Thomas was kept warm by his burning armor, but Mia was shivering.

He put his arms around her, protecting her from the winds. She stood that way, holding tight to him for several seconds before she looked up. "The High King said you would have something for me. Something that could save my life?"

He regarded her with wonder. "The High King spoke to you?"

A little contented smile spread on her lips. "He did."

"And the vision, you had the vision, didn't you?"

She breathed out a sigh, not of frustration, but as if the weight of it, the significance of it necessitated it. "Yes. He's more magnificent than you ever described. I understand now. So much of what you've done. Who you've been since pledging yourself to him."

Thomas's voice broke. "And you … did you yield to him? Are you?"

Mia grinned broadly and stepped back from him. She pointed to Hurstwell's spiritsword. "I believe that's what you were to bring me."

"Oh, um, right." He handed over the blade, hilt first. The blade's flames diminished to a glow.

The instant Mia wrapped her fingers around the hilt again, the flames flared back up its length, crackling in the snowy downpour.

It was everything Thomas had wanted for Mia. "Mia, you … When did you change your mind … about the Order?"

She took his hand and squeezed it gently. "I've been with you almost two years now. I've seen the difference in you. Loved the difference in you. After everything we've been through, it's changed the Lowlands for me—changed me."

A cry of fury echoed into the valley, loud enough to send a shudder through the mountains. The wyvern had emerged from its cavern where it had been kept dormant for who knew how many centuries and millennia. Kept in wait for this day, only to be denied its destiny. The beast took to the sky with a single thunderous flap of its enormous wings, displacing much of the snowfall around the entrance.

Below it, monarchist soldiers spewed out of the cave, some dashing straight for the camp, and therefore, Thomas and Mia. Others staggered, sizzling burns allotted them by the wyvern smoking in the frigid air. After them emerged Delia, looking as fierce as the blizzard around them. It was impossible to tell from this distance and through the snowfall to what she had affixed her gaze, but an easy guess was at the two of them. Her ire would be for Mia, in particular.

Thomas turned his attention to Mia. She had an intensity about her. As if all the Lowlands had focused on one point. "You're going to try to face Delia alone, aren't you?"

Her cheeks flushed a bit. "You know me better than anyone, save the High King."

"We can do it together. You aren't alone. I know the cuts she delivered run deep."

She nodded. Her lips pursed as if to hold in, hold back something. But she shook her head and her expression lightened. "I know you would die for me. But that isn't your battle, and I won't be alone. The High King goes with me everywhere." Mia held out the burning spiritsword in her hand as evidence.

"Then at least take the armor I have. It will protect you."

Mia leaned up and kissed him on the lips. A short but tender embrace.

He must have looked besmirched because a smirk, bittersweet, quirked up the corner of her mouth. "You're always taking care of me. And sweet as it may be, someone has to face that wyvern, and you're the only one with the skills and arms to do it."

The weight of the task apportioned him hit him then. She was right. If he didn't stop the beast, even if Delia was thwarted and no dragon was unleashed on the Lowlands, a wyvern left unchecked would eviscerate Albaron's heartland. After all the blows they'd weathered, that could be the one that finished them.

"I know you too," Mia noted a lilt of pleasure in her voice. "You won't fail."

"Neither will you," he replied, squeezing her hand.

She gave him another quick kiss and pulled away. At the tent entrance, she paused. "Did you ... have you ... read what I wrote in the proposal document?"

"No," he admitted. "I couldn't bring myself to till you're safe again."

She nodded, and as she stepped out of the tent entrance, she called, "I'll make sure to come back to you then. I've never let my sister win any of our games growing up, and I'm not about to let her win this now."

As if summoned by challenge, one of the Monarchist soldiers skidded to a halt on the snowy stone and turned to face them.

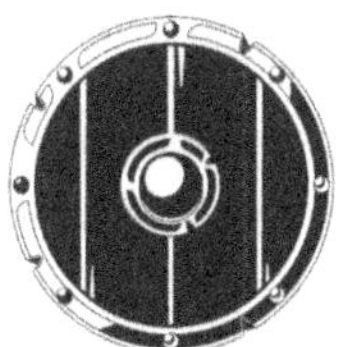

Thomas stepped forward and raised his sword. Its crackling flames filled the space between them with light.

The soldier's eyes went wide, fixed on the blade. He didn't move, didn't draw the sword sheathed at his hip. His chest heaved as he struggled to regain his breath.

Mia gripped Thomas's back and arm fiercely. He knew when the fight actually began, he'd be disadvantaged by it, but he couldn't fault her for feeling so startled by this bizarre encounter.

Suddenly, the Monarchist blinked and seemed to fully notice Thomas and Mia. His mouth hung open, and he started to speak, but a roar from the wyvern above cut him off. Staring upward at the beast, which was outside Thomas's view, the soldier dashed away.

Thomas peered around the tent and saw that the remaining Monarchists were fleeing. That wasn't at all what he had expected of them.

Mia cleared her throat and released her hold on Thomas's

arm. "Apparently, angry wyverns don't discern friends and foes."

"Maybe no wyverns do," Thomas offered. "I don't imagine dragons would care for the wiles of man, whatever delusions Monarch Ilyron may hold."

She fixed him with an intense stare. "Then do not give it any quarter. Not a breath's space to work its ill."

If only it were that simple.

He nodded all the same and looked toward where he'd last seen Delia. As if unaware or unconcerned about the furious wyvern flapping above, she stood there. She was waiting for them. Thomas could almost feel the bloodlust and fury radiating from her, and it sent a shiver down his back.

"There are soldiers of Albaron and Ecthelowall on the ridge above us," he pointed to where he'd left Ulster, Strathmore, and the others. If you need aid, fly to them, and they will render it."

After a second of searching him, Mia nodded. Probably humoring him. The odds were against either of them, surviving. Then again, hadn't they always been so ever since they took that fateful trip through Cromwell Forest?

With nothing left to say, Thomas watched as Mia backed away, into the snowstorm. His heart hammered as he saw her break into a run, dress billowing in the harsh wind as she raced toward her sister. The best he could do now for her was make sure those baleful ochre eyes of the wyvern were interminably on him. Looking around for some way to do that, he noticed the camp's fire.

Of course!

Gripping his spiritsword tight, he smiled appreciatively down at the burning blade and then proceeded to use it on the tent's fabric. In the span of a few seconds, the fire caught, and the flames spread.

Rushing from tent to tent, he set ablaze the whole camp. Thomas strode back several feet and held his hand over the eye slots of his helmet as he watched the fires burning.

"Eyarrgh!"

He swallowed back his anxiety and steeled himself. It worked. The wyvern had noticed too.

In case it was missing his challenge, he walked out into the open flat before the base of another of the jagged peaks lining the valley. Incautious. Brash. A whole host of criticisms for how he was handling this paged through his mind.

The one he settled on, though, was successful. His wyvern foe made another furious throaty sound and landed with a crash halfway up the snowy slope in front of Thomas. Leaning forward, it opened its huge jaws, and from them erupted a greenish blaze that seemed to darken the valley rather than light it.

Thomas realized the flames weren't just for a display. They arced over at him. Dropping to a crouch, he held his shield up just in time to block the unnatural flames. But the impact was stronger than he expected, and he slid backward along the snow-slicked ground.

Snow was flash evaporated into a mist that formed a blinding haze around him. All he could do was grit his teeth and hold firm, hearing and feeling the heat of the blast on the other side of his *Thyreos Pistis*. The shield impossibly bore up under the onslaught. As the blast continued without abating, it seemed impossible that the shield could endure it.

Under his breath, Thomas reminded himself, "No arrow or bolt has passed through its surface. No fire or acid can burn through to injure the Knight who allows it to be his defense." Anargen had confirmed that for him in their brief time together. How Thomas wished now it could have been longer. That he could have learned more, trained more, better prepared himself to face this foe. This devastating, beast that felled heroes of legend as surely as anyone else. A destructive power no army of the Lowlands could resist.

The pressure against the shield ended suddenly, and with it, the breathy, rushing sound of the wyvern's fire. It was so still. Had the wyvern fled? It sounded silly to think the massive beast sensed his resolve and feared it. There was no knowing. In the silence, Thomas was left with only his eyes to guide him in the battle, and they were little help with the thick mists created from the creature's fetid breath.

He moved forward in what he thought was a straight line, his shield held at the ready. Ahead, the mists cleared, and he could tell he'd wandered off his intended path.

Thump.

The ground shuddered around Thomas. A twinge of dread sent icy ripples throughout his body. He spun around and jerked his head upward. The wyvern was looming over him.

Its piercing screech made him want to cover his ears and dash away, never to return. He couldn't do that. Never mind that it would doom Mia, it could doom the whole Restoration if a wyvern struck Albaron's cities unchecked. Worse, if Delia actually did succeed in her ritual, legends said a dragon could destroy the entire Lowlands.

Thomas leaped to the left as the beast opened its enormous crocodilian jaws and lunged at him like a robin pecking at an earthworm. He rolled and took precious seconds, fumbling to get to his feet on the slippery surface.

The wyvern lowered its right wing and battered him aside.

Terrible seconds passed before he landed hard a dozen feet from where he had last stood. He felt like he had just taken a direct hit from a battering ram.

Thomas's body bounced and skittered along the icy plain until, at last, he came to a stop. Aches exploded from all over his body, and he shook with the effort of pushing himself up on one elbow after such a painful blow. The wyvern slowly advanced on him, its head twitching with quick snapping movements of an animal attentive for any disruptions to its impending meal.

Thomas looked toward where Mia was and saw that she, too, was on the ground. She wasn't moving, and Delia was advancing on her with the slow, confident stride of a victor.

They had been through so much, and each had lost more than seemed bearable. With Vif's arrival and Mia experiencing the vision, Thomas had secretly taken for granted they would be victorious. Unscathed by their foes. But out in the cold, swirling barrage of icy flakes and staring into those malignant ochre eyes of the wyvern—seeing the predatory stalking of Delia—it was so much more obvious that this was the end. They were going to die here, and the Lowlands would experience the devastating blow of their failure.

A shadow fell over Thomas. The wyvern loomed above, regarding him. Its tongue shot out, as if sampling the air. A low growl rumbled from its chest. His very existence must vex the creature.

Eyes narrowing, it reared back and snapped forward like a whip. Jaws opened wide to grab him up in one fell bite.

Mustering all his strength, Thomas heaved himself out of the way, rolling to the side and getting to his knees. It was enough to put him just behind and to the side of where the wyvern chomped. Seizing the opportunity, Thomas slashed at its jaw, leaving a glowing slice along the jade scales.

The beast reared back and screeched, thrashing its head from side to side. It stomped its feet in rage, forcing Thomas to dodge each ground-shaking step to avoid being crushed.

He managed to put enough distance between himself and the beast's feet that he could steady his ragged breathing and watch. The petulant display lasted almost a minute long.

Is this a young wyvern, or are they all this tempestuous by nature?

Though he could scarcely afford to do so, he spared a glance toward Mia. She was half crouched, half kneeled on the ground. One hand held the spiritsword pointing it in what looked like warning. Her other hand was on her abdomen. There was no telling from where he stood how bad whatever injury she sustained was, but he feared for her.

If she's bleeding from a wound—

A flicker of motion caught Thomas's attention. He spun back around. The wyvern's head was lowered and abruptly jerked it upward.

Thomas swung his shield around just in time as the prominent nose horn of the wyvern struck. Grinding against the stalwart argent shield, the impact sent him tumbling backward. A second's hesitancy and he would have been gored.

The enormous reptilian creature chomped after him. Quick punctuated snaps. Thomas twisted and dove out of the way of each, just managing to keep ahead of those wicked teeth.

A huff of hot air with a distinct sulfurous odor gusted from the wyvern's nostrils. Each clipped movement betrayed its building agitation. Thomas couldn't keep ahead of it forever. His body ached from the hits he'd taken. At some point, he would make a mistake, and that would be the end.

An instant later the beast missed snapping at him, and instead of rearing back and trying again, it swung its head around and bashed into Thomas, who hadn't yet gotten his feet set. The teen crashed through the snow once again.

He came to a stop beside the sizzling wreckage of one of the camp's tents. Poor cover, but it kept the beast from finishing him with a quick bite that sprayed him with caustic spittle.

Possibly poisonous, the spittle burned off Thomas's

divinely graced armor in seconds. About as long as his respite lasted. He flattened as the wyvern swept its great spiked tail around and bashed aside the charred tent remains, snapping the still standing sturdy wooden poles propping it like dried twigs.

Scrambling to his feet and holding his shield up in guard, Thomas looked up once more at his foe. The creature was squaring itself with him, planting each foot and arching its back as it had before. In a few seconds, an inferno carried on the beast's breath would envelop him. He was much closer this time than last. Thomas knew what was said of his shield that bore the High King's words inscribed on it, but how could it resist such a torrent?

The beast sucked in, and it felt like all of the breathable air was stolen from around Thomas. Eyes wide with fear, a whisper gripped his attention. It turned his attention to a glimmer running down the length of the spiritsword he held. On it, the lettering inscribed there glowed brighter across a section of the blade. In spite of how desperately he knew he need focus on the peril before him, he couldn't stop his eyes from following the letters and his mind from fixating on what it read:

"Be strong and courageous. Do not be frightened, and do not be dismayed, for the Hɪɢʜ Kɪɴɢ *is with you ..."*

Thomas whipped his head around to see the wyvern bearing down. A blast of green fire sped at him and crashed into his shield. The fire pushed him with much greater force and heat than the first time. His arm shuddered under the strength of it, threatening to buckle and drop his defense. All was lost in the vortex of flame. There was no snow left around him, not even moisture to slip on—it had all been flash-evaporated in an instant. Last time the blast came from so much farther away, so much less empowered by the wyvern. Withstanding it had been a feat. How could he hold on now? The fire was too much, too powerful for him to stand against.

No. Don't do that. Don't forget you've seen real fire. Real power. He chose you. Summoned you to his service. You're carrying his arms, his armor, and if he decrees this shield holds, then that beast has nothing it can do to overturn the High King's will.

Setting his feet, Thomas pushed back against the stream of fire smashing into him, fighting against it, resisting as he had the breakers of the Tislatnean Sea that had lapped onto the shores of his childhood home, the Isle of Fens. This wyvern, a remnant of that forsaken and utterly devastated ruin of Tislatna would not overcome him—would not overcome the one arming him, defending him, strengthening him for this struggle. The High King overturned an entire civilization of dragons. He would ensure Thomas stood firm against this poor facsimile now.

All at once, the fiery onslaught ended—a haze of acrid smoke roiling off the charred stone around him, much of it rendered molten. Thomas gasped and dropped to one knee. For all his resolve, he felt drained.

Across from him, the wyvern huffed exhausted breaths through its great snout, its ochre eyes wide now with something Thomas recognized—fear.

It fumbled back a step. If an animal could experience disbelief, this wyvern was enthralled by it. From the way it wobbled as it tried to put space between them, it had put its full measure of strength and fury into that blast. Apparently, wyvern were not accustomed to failure.

The whisper to press the attack was like a shout in Thomas's ears, and vaguely he wondered if he wasn't hearing a shout beyond himself as well. But he couldn't, his legs were as spent as the stone around him.

My King, I know you are with me. Help me finish the battle for your honor and people.

Heat flooded his limbs, filling them with the strength absent a moment before. Thomas leaped forward over the melted rock and sprinted up to the wyvern, delivering a glancing blow to the first of its legs he encountered. Though its scales were like ardent armor, they gave under the righteous, fiery fury of his blade.

Thomas didn't hesitate, dodging as the wyvern reeled from the pain. Coming to the other leg, he jammed his sword into its calf. This elicited shriek from the wyvern, and Thomas held on tight to the sword hilt as the creature thrashed. He extracted his sword at an angle, causing as much damage as he could.

Then he dashed to the side, as the beast's leg gave under its weight. It hit the ground with a groan.

Rushing up to it, Thomas scrambled onto its back and dodged past the sharp osteoderms on its spine. He only stopped when he reached where the thing's neck disappeared under its frilled crest at the back of its head. Guided to here, the weakest point on the menacing reptile, he hammered home his blade into that softened space until it sank to the hilt. Flames flared from the spiritsword, bright and hot, searing a creature by nature resistant to immense heat and fire.

The wyvern gave out a shrill cry, flailed futilely, and dropped its head.

In the stillness, Thomas's arms shook with the intensity of what had just happened. He didn't dare pull free his sword until he felt certain this was no ruse. The wyvern was dead.

Extracting his spiritsword, Thomas half fell, half jumped off its back, almost tripping on a crumpled winged arm that had landed at an unnatural angle.

He dropped to his knees and pulled up the faceplate of his helmet. Looking up, he closed his eyes. Each icy touch of the snowflakes as they melted on contact with his skin convinced him. This wasn't a dream. This wasn't deceit. This wasn't imagined. He was alive and had slain the wyvern that could have ended so many lives and devastated so much of Albaron.

Thank you, Great King. Thank you for letting me be a part of your victory.

A warmth enveloped him like a thick, wool blanket, blocking the cold and buffeting wind around him. Thomas relished it.

"Ayahhh!"

Thomas's eyes snapped open as a scream, loud as the wyvern's, echoed off the mountains, audible over the whipping winds. The warmth from before held him fast, holding him together as his heart thudded with the panicked realization that the cry had sounded like Mia's voice.

28

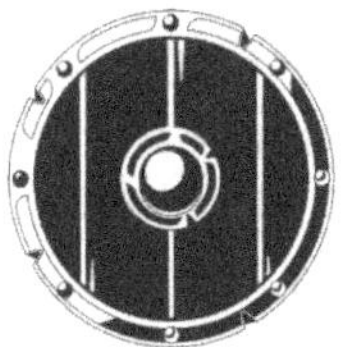

"Mia!" he tried to cry out. His throat felt choked off, closed to any sound. Thomas faltered as he attempted to stand. His legs were as though they were caught in the sea waves he had imagined earlier. He half-staggered, half-ran toward where the cry originated. Even in the blizzard's snowy haze, he could tell only one woman was left standing, and she was surrounded by a small grouping of soldiers.

No, no! Delia couldn't have had reinforcements.

Outnumbered, Mia hadn't stood a chance. How could he have let her face a twisted fiend like Delia alone?

His body protested now, having stepped out of the warmth ensconcing him moments ago. In the deeply buried rational part of his mind, he knew he couldn't take Delia and the soldiers alone. Perhaps not even Delia alone. In spite of his desire, he was sapped, too battered by this last blow to face what he must. But he couldn't stop himself either. Not even if it meant dying minutes after having just been part of such an incredible victory.

He slowed to a walk, conserving his strength, marshaling it, bracing himself for the fight ahead. As he neared, the snowy swirl around him lessened, as if the storm was finally passing on from here. By the time he reached the mouth of the cavern, he could see her looming over her fallen sister.

"Mia?" his croaked, a sob mangling a pitiful effort to speak.

She whirled around, one hand holding fast to her upper right arm to staunch a flow of blood from a wound there. In her limp arm, she still gripped Sir Hurstwell's spiritsword—*her* spiritsword.

"Thomas?" Her breathy question was heavy with as much trepid hope as his own.

Abandoning all caution for that hope, he sprinted to Mia and grabbed her in the tightest embrace of their lives. She winced under his hold, and he realized he was pressing on her injured arm. He pulled back. The apology ready on his lips was stifled by a kiss as Mia launched herself upward in the most frantic one he could ever remember them sharing. It was wild and sloppy, but he would take it and treasure it to his dying breath.

Thomas sheathed his sword and stroked Mia's cheek, pushing aside the damp, tangled red locks of her hair, still bearing up snowflakes like tiny auburn boughs of a tree. He stared into her eyes, unable to speak, unable to do anything but savor that she was here, before him. Alive. Both of them, alive. More than he believed possible for so long now.

"Ahem," one of the soldiers cleared his throat.

For an instant Thomas tensed and was about to pull Mia behind himself when he realized the soldiers before him weren't Monarchist reinforcements. They were from the Restoration. Sergeant Strathmore and Ulster and a few others of their group stood arrayed before them. At least ten of them were missing, and Thomas searched, finding all too quickly their fallen bodies strewn on the ground.

He swallowed against the sudden wave of guilt that washed over him. A bitter current amid the pure ecstasy he had been in a moment before. Thomas's gaze returned to Mia's and he could see her eyes glimmered with a mixture of the same turmoil of thankfulness and regret. At the edges, too, was her pain. Not just for her wound.

Of course, don't be a dolt. If she's alive and standing then the woman who cried out was Delia. No matter the evil that had twisted her, Delia was Mia's sister. Her only remaining family.

"It is good to see you well, sir," Strathmore said, moving over to grip the arm not wound around Mia protectively. "Sir Thomas Halifax, Wyvern's Bane ... ah, perhaps you'd like a kerchief?"

Rubbing at his nose with his free arm, Thomas realized that between the cold and the tears of joy that had run down his cheeks unbeknownst to him, he was a mess. His cheeks reddened under a flush of heat. It felt silly to be embarrassed by anything, particularly when he saw that Mia was just as wrecked as him. He nodded and a damp one was produced from somewhere.

He first offered it to Mia and then tended to himself. As he did, one of the missing soldiers emerged from deeper in the ranks, Ulster it happened, and examined Mia's arm. The stalwart Albaron quickly tended to it, expertly applying a compress and makeshift binding of sorts to it.

"Are all of Albaron's children healers?" Thomas quipped numbly.

Ulster's lip curled up in confusion as he regarded Thomas like he might a jester who had wandered over to take a Steward's seat as his own.

This elicited a hearty chuckle from Strathmore that spread amongst the group, and Thomas felt even more abashed. With all the tumult of emotion and action that had beset them, he was almost dizzy. It would be best for him to listen more and speak less until he had steadied himself.

Mia leaned against him, and he shored up his footing to make sure he could support her. Glancing down at her, he followed her gaze to Delia's body. Little tendrils of smoke still emanated from a pair of wounds. One glancing, one fatal.

Strathmore must have noticed the object of their focus. "Begging your pardon, Baroness. We should try to get a fire started and camp made. Then we'll see to a proper burial."

Thomas felt Mia bury her face in his side. A little shudder ran through her body. He tightened his hold on her, worried she might be going into shock. After a few seconds, she turned her head back to face the others and said in a voice steadier than he was sure he could manage, "Thank you, Sergeant. See to your fallen first. They deserve greater honor."

Strathmore nodded. "Thank you, Baroness." Turning slightly to Ulster, he said, "You should find your brother and the others and bring them back. Capturing the other Monarchists is a lesser priority."

Ulster nodded without a word and headed toward the northwest, the direction the Monarchists had fled. He moved as swiftly as a goat over the snow and uneven stone. The Albaron was out of sight before Thomas could broach the question raised by Strathmore's instruction. "Fenwick and his group pursued the Monarchists fleeing the wyvern. You and your men ...?"

"They rescued me," Mia supplied hastily, her eyes still on Delia. "My sister had me down, ready to carve me up as a sacrifice to that beast. The Sergeant and the others came down from the mountainside and ambushed her ..."

Strathmore picked up as Mia's voice trailed off. "Even with all of us brought to bear, the Queen's sorcery was—" he hesitated, rubbing at a spot where his chest plate and pauldron met. Thomas noticed now there was a scorch mark there as if he'd been struck by lightning. "Terrifying. We did what we could, but it was the Baroness who saved us all. I didn't realize we had two Knights of Light among us today."

His wearied eyes roved over each of them. There was something there—jealousy, longing, maybe? Thomas got the impression that the Sergeant had a firm, healthy respect for the Order. But perhaps he viewed it as a thing to be won over a mercy to receive. A conquest instead of surrendering.

"Strathmore," Thomas began.

The other waved him off. "Begging your pardon, sir. I need to get to ordering the camp and dolling out tasks for the rest of us. You," he glanced from Thomas to Mia and back, "both deserve some time to yourselves."

With that, Strathmore and the other members of their rescue party headed off to the scorched and broken remains of the Monarchist camp. After a few minutes, they looked to be making quick progress, setting about the very ordinary and menial task of replacing it with their own.

"I suppose I've never been much of a soldier," Thomas noted, as he observed them.

Mia, who was still leaning against him again, commented absently, "Why would you say that?"

"Look at them. After seeing a wyvern and a witch ..." he swallowed hard, having incautiously labeled Delia a witch in front of Mia. "And losing so many of their own, they're busy building an encampment. I feel like I'm barely holding together, and I'm a Knight of Light. I have the High King's hand to hold me, to strengthen me."

"We do," she affirmed. "And we have each other."

She looked away from her sister's body for the first time in a long while. It immediately drew Thomas's attention back to her. Mia's emerald eyes shimmered with barely held-back tears. Beneath those tears, however, was heat and resolve. A sea, deep and beautiful.

"What we lost, though, is more personal. They lost comrades. We lost family. They risked defeat in war, we risked losing everything we hold dear in the Lowlands."

Thomas was tempted to argue the point. Grief was not so simple as if on a sliding scale of bad to worst. Recalling how he'd felt after losing his parents, though, he could not bring himself to say that. Not when Mia's heart was ravaged by this loss. Instead, he spoke on the torrent of his emotions.

"Would that you had never faced this day. That you had been spared all the hurt and heartache the Lowlands holds. You deserve better."

Mia shook her head. "No, I really don't."

"Mia?"

She offered him a somber smile and brushed his cheek with her fingertips. "Now that I've seen the High King for myself, I understand. The Lowlands reflect what our rebellion begets. We are reaping what we and generations before us sowed. Bitter and hard as the fruits are, they are our fruits.

"You know, you showed me that by how different you were after becoming a Knight of Light, while still being you. There was a different sort of fruit you cultivated. Maybe if Delia and I hadn't been so stubborn, been so convinced of our place and purpose as nobles and heirs of all that the Lowlands is now, we would've both realized rebellion's cost and that we need not perish as its price. Not when the High King absolves those debts when we yield to him."

Thomas drew in a breath and let it out slowly. "You're

right, of course. I wish I had your poise right now. I could hardly hope to say I've ever handled anything so well."

Pulling back from him, she shook her head. "I watched you with Sir Hurstwell's passing. He was the closest thing to a real father that you had and died a noble death, fighting evil. That feels so much more tragic than Delia's passing. Dying a witch, who had forsaken everyone she cared about for her temporary gain. Right up until the end, she was cursing me and promising me she would kill you and everyone else in her way. That she'd make me suffer until she snuffed me out by forcing me to watch it happen. And I wanted her gone. I wanted her—"

Mia's steady hold on her emotions broke, and she looked away as the tears ran fresh and hot. She wiped them away, but more came. Her tenuous poise broke, and she crumpled, a wail caught in her throat.

Catching Mia and steadying her, Thomas held her close and stroked her back, as he'd done the night after Delia first revealed her true nature and murdered their father. This is what they did. They held each other together against the hurt, amid the evil. He believed the High King had brought them to each other for that reason. Now wasn't the time to tell her that. For all the wise and deep elucidating she'd just done, the pain was still too raw. She didn't need the deep and complex realities at work around them. Those they could work through in time. Instead, he gave her the thing he could most freely, "You didn't want Delia to die. Only the evil in her. This wasn't your fault. If anything, you becoming a Knight, embracing the light, was one last clarion call for her to turn back from the path she'd freely chosen."

Through reddened eyes, she blinked, regarding him. Without a word, she reached up a kissed him. This time tender, gentle. As their lips parted, she gripped onto him tighter like he was a rock keeping her safely out of a tempest-tossed sea around her. And he clung right back to her, because amidst the devastation that had beset them, they had persevered—by the High King's favor—and though tomorrow wasn't certain, they were much stronger. Much better equipped to face what still lay ahead.

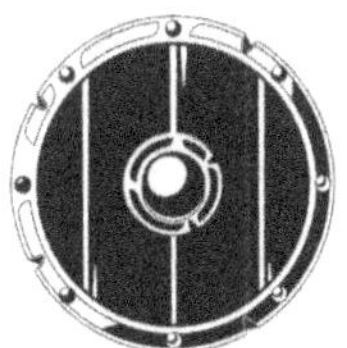

This room, small, stuffy as it was, and utterly dark, suited Thomas as well as any. Tugging at the vest he wore, he chaffed under the finery he had been given to wear. It was one part of living as a noble he had not missed in all these years. Even less so now, having just sat through the funeral for the second man to attempt to adopt him.

First Sir Hurstwell. Now Viceroy Ecthelion.

With each was something more than just losing a father and mentor. They were brothers, members of the Knights of Light, and to lose anyone in the Order was to lose the closest of family. When they'd returned from Wyvares, he hadn't had more than a few moments with Ecthelion before he passed. All he had said was, "Ordumair. Dual springs. Two peoples, one purpose. Keep the Tower alight."

Thomas hadn't the faintest idea what Ecthelion meant. He knew of Ordumair from his people's history. The dwarfs that lived there had until recently been bitter rivals with Ecthelowall. It was at Ordumair that Ecthelion had been first betrayed by Ilyron. It was also there that Ecthelion made peace with the Ords after centuries of war. But the Viceroy's words hardly felt like a proclamation of his greatest achievement for an epitaph, they were more like an adjuration. A warning of sorts, even.

"You know you won't always be able to sneak away from such things," a gentle voice soothed from the doorway.

He looked over his shoulder and then turned fully to face Mia. Light streamed in from beyond the doorway, shining on her long ruddy curls and over her gown, dower and subdued as it was by virtue of the purpose. She was staggeringly beautiful. Her sister Delia had once been so, too, but what he loved most about Mia was discovering that her inward beauty exceeded even that of her outward.

"I'm favored by the High King then to have you always there to rescue me."

A smile turned up the corner of her mouth and she shook her head. "What was I thinking, agreeing to marry you?"

His eyes widened, his hand drifting to where the parchment for his proposal was kept tucked away. With everything that happened, he hadn't been able to bring himself to look at it. Here he was just hearing it for the first time, and was Mia already having regrets?

No. He could see it clearly gleaming within her gaze. She was his, and he hers, until the very end. The question had been purely rhetorical, and Thomas was glad for that, because honestly, he had no reasonable answer in worldly terms, though one thing did express a deeper truth. "As I said, I'm favored by the High King. Immeasurably."

"As am I," she said, crossing the room and locking her wrists behind his neck. She pulled him down so that their foreheads touched. More tenderly, earnestly, she asked, "How are you, really?"

He closed his eyes. This was what they did. Held each

other together. Him holding her in Wyvares over Delia. Her holding him here in Caldoness over Ecthelion. "I'll live," he said. "As long as the other barons stop glaring daggers at me every time they address me as Baron Halifax. In fact, I'd be fine with them just ignoring me altogether. They act as if I conned the Viceroy into adopting me and bequeathing me his title."

Mia gave a little shrug. "You can't tell me you forgot how petty the nobility—or people generally, for that matter—can be?"

He mimicked her shrug. "I suppose not."

"Besides," she grinned broadly. "You most certainly aren't forgetting that it's thanks to his adopting you that we can be together without causing a scandal ..."

She reached up and brushed his lips with a kiss that was maddeningly brief and yet exquisitely satisfying. "That is one part of being his heir I will never regret."

"Good." She let her hands drift down to hold his, a conspiratorial gleam in her eyes. "Me either."

If someone had told him this would be his life a couple of years ago, he'd have called them mad. Unequivocally, frothing mad. Yet it didn't feel like a dream or hallucination. It felt like following a river along its natural course, even if the rapids and bends had not been anticipated. Even if a year ago this hadn't seemed what lay ahead in the slightest.

"Come on," he said, pulling out of his introspection. "We better get back out there before I cause a greater stir by making everyone think I'm trying to steal your virtue."

"Ahem," someone cleared their throat from the doorway to the little scullery room.

Well, I suppose that's exactly what's happening. Great.

Mia had the good sense to reply. "Yes? What is it?"

Sergeant Strathmore stepped in, newly promoted to Captain. "Baron, Baroness. I apologize for, er, interrupting."

Cocking her head to the side, Mia said, "Not at all, Captain. I was simply retrieving my fiancé. He is a bit rusty regarding protocol at events of state."

The captain's eyes widened, and he shot Thomas a look of congratulation. "As you say it, Lady Sornfold," he replied. His good humor was short-lived however, and his face quickly settled back into something heavier, melancholy, burdened.

"Is something the matter, Captain?" Thomas asked.

Strathmore reached across the space to hand over a sealed parchment scroll. The wax was the dark green of the Monarchists' banner and with only a cursory glance, Thomas recognized it to be Maldes Ilyron's personal signet stamped into it.

"Monarch Ilyron sent me a parchment? How? Why?"

"It arrived by a neutral courier this evening. As to its contents, I cannot say," Strathmore said with a bounce of his bushy brows. "I thought to pass it on to you after tonight's ceremony, but, after all we've been through, I didn't want to delay."

Thomas shot a glance at Mia, who simply furrowed her brows in a way that looked like she was concerned that breaking the seal might break him. He gave her hand a squeeze of reassurance, undid the wax, and unrolled the document. He read aloud,

"Maldes Ilyron, son Ecthelion Halifax, Monarch of Ecthelowall, Baron of Halifax, Baron of Emeral, Prince of the Middlebane Islands, to Sir Thomas Fenwrest self-styled Baron of Halifax and Lady Mia Sornfold self-styled Baroness of Emeral:

"Greetings to you each, sent on this, the eve marking the official start of your regencies. May hale days ever watch o'er your joined houses."

Thomas shot Mia a look. How could he have known about them?

"You are no doubt wondering what manner of letter has arrived to you from your Monarch. Given you each have usurped a title belonging to your sovereign, it would only be right and proper to remind you of the cost of treason. This letter should be arriving just as they are laying under a stone lid the leader of the rebellious Restoration movement. With Ecthelion Halifax's passing, his title duly falls to his surviving heir, Maldes Ilyron. Likewise, as this letter is penned, a similar ceremony has just concluded in memoriam for Delia Sornfold, Queen of Ecthelowall, Baroness of Emeral, Princess of the Middlebane Islands. With her passing, her title to Emeral duly falls to her surviving husband, Maldes Ilyron and a warrant for the arrest of her murderers has been drafted for distribution across Ecthelowall's imperial domain. As you may surmise, you are both fate-spoken ... but you need not stay so.

"Indeed, you each at present face a despicable fate, including a most ignoble death in the public square of Ecthalon. However, your sovereign is not without mercy nor gratitude. You see the Queen, while lovely to behold, was treacherous, as you yourselves are aware. Moreover, she was bitter, rotted through the core, to our deepest regret. Thus, her passing has remarkably simplified plans long laid. Though the loss of the juvenile wyvern she foolishly attempted to free and empower as the first dragon in millennia is regrettable, that young and unimpressive specimen is by no means the only exemplar of its species left in the Lowlands. There remains two wyvern, each long trapped deep within the mountains south of Wyvares—in Fiorsruthain, the mountain of Ordumair, to be direct. The imperial army marches even now on Ordumair to lay claim to these two creatures, the birthright of Ecthelowall as the heir of the Lost Realm of Tislatna's glorious heritage and ways. Which presents an opportunity for you each to rewrite the fates spoken over you. Should you ensure that none of Albaron's armies attempt interference in the conflict that must inevitably take place at Ordumair, you will both be spared and rewarded with the titles you usurped, permitted under the auspices of your sovereign to consummate your relationship and join your houses as a part of the new Empire of Ecthelowall. Such benevolence was once offered by the former Queen in jest as a cruelty, however, your sovereign does not share the former Queen's indulgence in callous pettiness. Thus, you may count as assured this guarantee of your reward. A simple task for two such intrepid children of the former noble houses of Ecthelowall. Failure to embrace this opportunity will see the dispersal of the warrant aforementioned and the ignoble death—filled with pains to properly instruct those witnessing in the costs of treason—will be carried out swiftly and without delay or remediation.

"As your sovereign believes actions speak far louder than mere words, and the vicissitudes of what lays before you are plain, you need not write a reply. You may simply act in accordance with the fate presented before you and of your greatest desire, understanding, no matter what you choose, three things will hold constant. Firstly, Ordumair will fall. Second, the ancient rites to produce the dragons in service to the sovereign will be created. Last, the Restoration and all nations, orders, and individuals constituting that illegal and treasonous movement shall be utterly destroyed.

"Maldes Ilyron,

Monarch of Ecthelowall, Baron of Halifax, Baron of Emeral, and Prince of the Middlebane Islands

Daraleath 29 1608"

Thomas stared at the parchment for several seconds after he finished reading it aloud. He then very slowly rolled up the scroll, such that if the wax had not had the fissures running along it from its break, it would have looked as though he'd never read it.

"Such heartfelt sentiments from such a black heart," Mia commented, every word barbed with ire.

"Your Honors are under no obligation to share your inner counsels," Strathmore began, his words spoken with great caution, "But I'm afraid I'll need to report this to Council of Barons and the Laird of Albaron."

Mia scowled furiously at Strathmore, "Do you honestly believe we intend to comply with that madman's demands?"

Strathmore swallowed uncomfortably, his eyes resting heavily on the still silent Thomas. "Begging your pardon, Your Honors. No disrespect is intended, but to be frank, you are both very young, and I know how close your love came to being fate-spoken. Here now it seems to once more be proven to be so. No one would be ... what I'm trying to say is ... You ought to understand—"

"Ilyron is offering a quick and easy path to safeguard what we have, to seize our destiny, to master our fates," Thomas mused distantly.

"Precisely," Strathmore agreed. "And that has to be a tempting offer."

"Arrgh," huffed Mia. "I can't believe you think we're so oblivious. Ilyron gave us a written letter with his plans in it. He isn't such a fool that he would do so knowing the courier was instructed to hand the letter off to anyone besides one of us."

"I don't follow," Strathmore admitted.

"He already knows what we choose," Thomas replied, finally focused again. "By giving the letter through courier to you to deliver, he knows you will have to report its contents. So, unless we truly are murderers and kill you to keep you quiet, his plans will be known irrespective of our choice, and therefore, our choice doesn't matter."

Strathmore's brows furrowed, "He's just trying to taint and torment you? Because he already believes he's won."

"Yes," Mia said, gesturing with exasperation heightened no doubt by the stress the letter induced. She paced in the confined space, her hands on the small of her back as mumbled possible recourses.

Thomas took her hand. "Mia," he soothed.

"Mia." He repeated it finally gaining her attention. In her eyes was fear, sorrow, as if she already were considering them both dead, everything lost. Which was exactly what the letter implied.

"Ilyron had his chance and unleashed all the devastation in his power upon us, but by the High King's favor we stood firm. We are battered, bruised, bleeding, but we aren't broken. We aren't beaten. And if we are fate-spoken, that fate was decreed by the High King of All Realms."

Mia's chin drifted down, tears forming in the corner of her eyes. Thomas lifted up her chin so her eyes were on his again as he finished. "I understand now what the Viceroy's last words to me meant, and we need only have courage to follow the High King through the hard things that lay ahead."

ACKNOWLEDGMENTS

No two books are the same, and neither is the experience of writing them. There are highs, and there are lows. Through them all, my family has supported me through the very hardest moments, and without them, *Devastation* likely wouldn't have made it to completion.

I owe an enormous thank you to my publisher, Linda Fulkerson. Quest of Fire hasn't been a sprint, and I rarely hit deadlines the way I should. But she has been incredibly patient and encouraging in a way that every author hopes for and needs from their publisher. Along with Linda, Erin Howard has been a huge part of shaping the series with her insightful edits.

Both my bosses, Andrew Neely and Daniel Mead, have been incredibly supportive and flexible with my work time. Writing by night doesn't always lend enough hours, and they have been enormously gracious with letting me take the time I need to craft stories like *Devastation*.

To all those who have read and shared their thoughts on my books or spoken a kind word, thank you. It's easy to get battered in publishing, and each act of encouragement helps to keep me getting up from the trips and pitfalls and striving to go farther, do better.

Last, and most of all, all my thanks and praise belong to the LORD. My prayer is always to be a brush in His skilled hand,

and I am never a worthy tool. Never as refined or compliant as the art He would make through me deserves. But He continues to draw me to stories and show me with each a little bit more of Himself and allows me to share that with others. To God be all the glory.

ABOUT THE AUTHOR

Brett Armstrong has been exploring other worlds as a writer since age nine. Years later, he still writes, but now invites others along on his excursions. He's shown readers haunting, deep historical fiction (*Destitutio Quod Remissio*), scary-real dystopian sci-fi (*Tomorrow's Edge*) and dark, sweeping epic fantasy (*Quest of Fire*). Every story is a journey of discovery and an attempt to be a brush in the Master Artist's hand. Through dark, despair, light, joy, and everything in between, the end is always meant to leave his fellow literary explorers with wonder and hope. Always busy with a new story, he also enjoys drawing, gardening, and spending time with his wife and son.

MORE FROM THE QUEST OF FIRE

The Gathering Dark

Quest of Fire Series – Book One

2020 Selah Awards Finalist

After a thousand years of light, a teen's world teeters on the edge of utter darkness.

On the run from his past, Jason hides in an inn where he hears a tale from centuries past about Anargen, a teen on a quest to bring peace between Ecthelowall's men and Ordumair's dwarfs. But an arcane evil seeks to ruin the peace talks and ensure a lost dwarf treasure isn't found by those for whom it's meant. As he listens, Jason realizes the story is more than a fable and he must choose whether to join Anargen's quest, which has shaped and can destroy his world.

Get your copy here: scrivenings.link/thegatheringdark

Succession: *A Novella*

Quest of Fire Series – Book Two

The heir must prove his worth - or die trying

Son of the Northern Realm's Defender, raised among the dwarves of Ordumair, Meredoch was anticipated to succeed his father. Some whispered he would bring the longed-for peace between Ordumair and their ancient foe, Ecthelowall. All of that changes when Ordumair's Thane is killed and Meredoch and his family are exiled.

From prestige to poverty, the young boy must chart a new course. Battling creatures believed only myths and racing against evil toward the prize, Meredoch must face the truth of his place in the world and claim his right of succession.

Get your copy here: scrivenings.link/succession

Shadows at Nightfall

Quest of Fire - Book Three

The hour has arrived ... with all its terrors.

The shadows of Jason's past have caught him. Having stepped into the Quest of Fire, Jason is pursued by a league of assassins formed of pure darkness. To his horror he discovers these creatures were also contracted to eliminate Anargen and his friends as they sought to understand the Tower of Light's oracle. To unravel the mystery of who wants him dead and how he fits into the ages old quest, Jason must travel the lengths of the Lowlands. He'll have to move fast, the darkest creatures in the Lowlands have long waited for this hour. With few concerned for the light and everything falling apart around them, Jason and Anargen will face the shadows of night's falling as their world hangs in the balance.

Get your copy here: https://scrivenings.link/shadowsatnightfall

Desperation: A Novella

Quest of Fire - Book Four

Guarding his nation's last hope, a teen must escape enemy lands.

While Anargen, Caeserus, and Bertinand are held captive in Stormridge, the war to restore Ecthelowall's Commonwealth has been waged for months. Enter Thomas Fenwrest, an orphan and page to the captain of Baron Fenwrest's guard and tasked with escorting the children of Restoration nobility to safety at Castle Yerst. Things quickly spiral out of control when the Monarchists deliver a devastating blow to the Restoration. Ancient sorcery and bitter grudges combine to ensnare them. As desperation sets in for the Restoration and Thomas, to where will they turn for hope?

Get your copy here: https://scrivenings.link/desperation

Resurgence of Dawn

Quest of Fire - Book Five

Hope returns with the dawn.

Haunted by tragedies and failures, Anargen and Jason each struggle to find their way. Night has fallen in the Lowlands and neither teen has an easy road ahead. In Anargen's Era, Monarch Ilyron's powers and influence grow, forcing Anargen and his dwindling list of allies to travel the length of the Lowlands in a desperate attempt to keep the Quest and all they hold dear from falling into ruin.

Jason meanwhile must find Aria and her grandfather to help unite the Knights of Light from across the Lowlands against his brother, Dorian. But agents of darkness and painful vestiges of his past mix with vindictive new enemies to make the hope of seeing the dawn of the longed-for King's Day ever so faint. If either teen gives in and surrenders, doom will come swiftly on their world.

https://scrivenings.link/resurgenceofdawn

ALSO BY BRETT ARMSTRONG

Day Moon

Tomorrow's Edge Trilogy Book One

AD 2039: Eluding authorities, one teen holds the past and future's key.

AD 2039: Project Alexandria is an initiative to give all humanity safe and equal access to all recorded knowledge. But the prodigious teen Elliott knows something is wrong. There are dark intentions behind Project Alexandria and the key may lie in the last print copy of Shakespeare's complete works that contains a sonnet titled, "Day Moon." Racing along a path made perilous by federal agents and betrayals from those closest to him, Elliott must uncover the sonnet's secrets. All of history past and to be depends on it.

Get your copy here: https://scrivenings.link/daymoon

Veiled Sun: *Tomorrow's Edge Trilogy Book Two*

2021 Selah Awards Finalist

AD 2040: Every day the world slips further into lies.

AD 2040: Every day the world slips further into lies. Seventeen-year-old Elliott knows that better than most. Project Alexandria is rewriting history, shaping the world according to sinister goals. To stop it, Elliott must assemble the "Veiled Sun", a secret program written by his grandfather.

The only people he can count on are siegers—outlaws who use their coding skills for purposes almost as nefarious as Project Alexandria. Overcoming the schemes and betrayals all around him, he's the world's best hope to save reality, if he doesn't lose hold of it himself.

Get your copy here: https://scrivenings.link/veiledsun

Silent Stars: *Tomorrow's Edge Trilogy Book Three*

AD 2040: Past and future hang in the balance as the stars fall silent.

AD 2040: Barely eighteen, things have become much harder for Elliott. Reeling from the losses during the confrontation that brought Project Alexandria to a halt. Elliott feverishly hunts for the original files needed to finish it off. Finding only dead ends, he instead stumbles upon something dire: messages about the Babel Initiative.

Conceived as a successor that would make Project Alexandria's manipulations seem tame, this new threat once again forces Elliott into alliances with morally grey programmers known as siegers. Beset by continual setbacks and defeats, many siegers abandon the cause and go underground to survive the dangers ahead.

The bleak reality that Elliott and those closest to him are almost certain to die in the fight against Dr. Almundson begins to set in. But Elliott isn't ready to give in. He knows the cost of such a silent surrender will be humanity itself.

Get your copy here: https://scrivenings.link/silentstars

The Near Distant—Novella Collection

by Brett Armstrong, Erin R. Howard, and

C. Kevin Thompson

Awards for "By Far and Away" by Brett Armstrong:

2023 Selah Awards Finalist

2023 Realm Awards Finalist

2023 Carol Awards Semi-Finalist

On a day trip into the wilderness around Lake Tahoe, college students Ned, Tyler, and Everly stumble upon a monolith. No one knows its origin or purpose, but structures like this one have popped up all over the world, making national headlines. While not the local legend the group hoped to find, they decide to investigate, only to be engulfed by a blinding, powerful pulse of light. Instantly, the three friends find themselves in separate and drastically different worlds. They must quickly adapt to their new surroundings or perish.

Get your copy here: https://scrivenings.link/theneardistant

Stay up-to-date on your favorite books and authors with our free e-newsletters.

ExpanseBooks.pub (an imprint of Scrivenings Press LLC)